红狐丛书·东亚卷 | 北岛 主编

The Metaphor of the Sea

海的比喻

海の比喩

Shuntarō Tanikawa

［日］谷川俊太郎 著 田原 译

江苏凤凰文艺出版社
JIANGSU PHOENIX LITERATURE AND ART PUBLISHING

目录

Contents

The Metaphor of the Sea

Shuntarō Tanikawa

生きる

生かす
六月の百合の花が私を生かす
死んだ魚が生かす
雨に濡れた仔犬が
その日の夕焼が私を生かす
生かす
忘れられぬ記憶が生かす
死神が私を生かす
生かす
ふとふりむいた一つの顔が私を生かす
愛は盲目の蛇
ねじれた臍の緒
赤錆びた鎖
仔犬の腕

活着

活着
六月的百合花让我活着
死去的鱼让我活着
被雨淋湿的狗崽
和那天的晚霞让我活着
活着
无法忘却的记忆让我活着
死神让我活着
活着
猛然回首的一张脸让我活着
爱是盲目的蛇
是扭结的脐带
是生锈的锁
是狗崽的脚脖

Living

They let me live.
A lily in June lets me live.
A dead fish lets me live.
A puppy wet with rain
and the evening glow that day let me live.
They let me live.
Unforgettable memories let me live.
The god of death lets me live.
They let me live.
A face suddenly facing me lets me live.
Love is a blind serpent,
a twisted umbilical cord,
a rusty chain,
a puppy's paws.

(Translated by William I. Elliott & Kazuo Kawamura)

鳥

鳥は空を名づけない
鳥は空を飛ぶだけだ
鳥は虫を名づけない
鳥は虫を食べるだけだ
鳥は愛を名づけない
鳥はただふたりで生きてゆくだけだ

鳥は歌うことを知っている
そのため鳥は世界に気づかない
不意に銃声がする
小さな鉛のかたまりが鳥を世界からひき離し鳥を人に結びつける
そして人の大きな嘘は鳥の中でつつましい真実になる
人は一瞬鳥を信じる
だがその時にさえ人は空を信じない
そのため人は鳥と空と自らを結ぶ大きな嘘を知らない
人はいつも無知に残されて
やがて死の中で空のために鳥にされる
やっと大きな嘘を知り　やっとその嘘の真実なのに気づく

鳥は生を名づけない
鳥はただ動いているだけだ
鳥は死を名づけない
鳥はただ動かなくなるだけだ
空はただいつまでもひろがっているだけだ

空はただいつまでもひろがっているだけだ

鸟

鸟无法给天空命名
鸟只是在天空飞翔
鸟无法给虫子命名
鸟只是啄食虫子
鸟无法给爱情命名
鸟只是成对地活下去

鸟谙熟歌声
为此，鸟觉察不到世界
突如其来的枪声
小小的铅弹使鸟和世界分离
也使鸟和人连结
于是，人类的弥天大谎在鸟群中变得谦恭与真实
人类瞬间笃信着鸟
但就连在此时，人类都不会相信天空
因此，人类不知道与鸟、天空和自己连结一起的谎言
人类总是被留在无知里
终将在死亡中，因天空而蜕变成鸟
才会看清那谎言的真貌

鸟无法给活着命名
鸟只是飞上飞下
鸟无法为死亡命名
鸟只是变得无法动弹

天空只是永恒地宽广

Birds

Birds don't name the sky.
Birds only fly in the sky.
Birds don't name insects.
Birds only eat insects.
Birds don't name love.
Birds only live in pairs.

Birds know how to sing
so they don't notice the world.
A sudden report of a gun—
tiny lead pellets tear birds from the world and bind them
to people,
and man's big lie becomes a humble truth in the birds.
Man believes the birds for a moment,
but even then he doesn't believe the sky.
So man doesn't believe the big lie that binds him to sky
and birds.
Man remains forever ignorant,
and, finally in his death, is changed into a bird because of
the sky.
At last he knows the big lie, and for the first time realizes
the truth of that lie.

Birds don't name life.
Birds only keep moving.
Birds don't name death.
Birds just stop moving.

The sky merely goes on expanding.

(Translated by William I. Elliott & Kazuo Kawamura)

愛について

私はみつめられる私
私は疑わせる私
私はふりむかせる私
私は見失われた私
そして私は愛ではない

私は心の中に逃げた肉
地を知らぬ足
心を投げられぬ手
心にみつめられた眼
そして私は愛ではない

私は陽の終った真昼
振り付けられた劇
名づけられた睦言
狎れすぎた暗闇
そして私は愛ではない

私は見知らぬ悲しみ
餓えている歓び
むすばれるものを選ぶ孤り
幸せの外の不幸せ
そして私は愛ではない

私は最もやさしい眼差
私はありあまる理解
私は erected penis
私は絶えない憧れ
そして私は愛ではないのだ

关于爱

我是被凝视的我
我是令人怀疑的我
我是让人回首的我
我是被迷失的我
但我不是爱

我是逃奔到心中的肉体
是不知道大地的脚
是无法扔掉心的手
是被心凝视的眼
但我不是爱

我是太阳滚过的正午
是被导演的一场戏
是被命名的闺房话
是司空见惯的黑暗
但我不是爱

我是看不见的悲伤
是充满渴望的欢愉
是选择被结合的一个人
是幸福之外的不幸
但我不是爱

我是最温柔的目光
我是多余的理解
我是勃起的阳具
我是不断的憧憬
但我绝不是爱

On Love

I am I, stared at by myself.
I am I, who make myself doubt me.
I am I, who make myself look back at me.
I am I, who've been lost sight of by myself.
And I am not Love.

I am flesh that has fled into my heart,
a foot unfamiliar with earth,
a hand that cannot hurl my heart,
eyes gazed at by my heart.
And I am not Love.

I am mid-day at the close of sunlight,
a play that is choreographed,
amorous words that have been named,
a too intimate darkness.
And I am not Love.

I am a sadness I don't know,
a famished joy,
a loneliness that chooses one I'll be united with,
an unhappiness outside of happiness.
And I am not Love.

I am a most affectionate eye.
I am an excessive understanding.
I am an erect penis.
I am an endless longing.
And, clearly, I am not Love.

(Translated by William I. Elliott & Kazuo Kawamura)

空

空はいつまでひろがっているのか
空はどこまでひろがっているのか
ぼくらの生きている間
空はどうして自らの青さに耐えているのか

ぼくらの死のむこうにも
空はひろがっているのか
その下でワルツはひびいているのか
その下で詩人は空の青さを疑っているのか

今日子供たちは遊ぶのに忙しい
幾千ものじゃんけんは空に捨てられ
なわとびの輪はこりずに空を計っている

空は何故それらのすべてを黙っているのか
何故遊ぶなと云わないのか
何故遊べと云わないのか

青空は枯れないのか
ぼくらの死のむこうでも
もし本当に枯れないのなら
枯れないのなら
青空は何故黙っているのか

ぼくらの生きている間
街でまた村で海で
空は何故
ひとりで暮れていってしまうのか

天空

天空能宽广到何时？
天空能宽广到何地？
我们活着的时候
天空为什么能忍受着自己的碧蓝？

我们死去的世界
天空还那么宽广吗？
在它下面，华尔兹舞曲还在奏响吗？
在它下面，诗人还会怀疑天空的碧蓝吗？

今天的孩子们忙于玩耍
数千次地把剪包锤的小拳头划向天空
跳绳的圈儿又不断地测量着天空

天空为什么对一切保持着沉默？
为什么不说你们别玩儿了
又为什么不说你们玩儿吧

蓝天不会枯竭吗？

即使在我们死去的世界

如果真的不会枯竭

不枯竭的话

蓝天为什么沉默着呢？

我们活着的时候

在大街、在乡村、在海边

天空为什么

独自地由白天转入黑夜？

The Sky

How long will the sky keep on expanding?
How far will the sky keep on expanding?
While we keep on living,
how can the sky stand its own blue?

Does the sky continue expanding
beyond our death?
Does a waltz go on being played beneath the sky?
Does a poet go on doubting the blue of the sky?

Today children are busy playing.
Thousands of rock-scissors-paper are being thrown
against the sky
and circling jump ropes are tirelessly measuring the sky.

Why is the sky silent about all these things?
Why doesn't it say, "Stop playing!"?
Why doesn't it say, "Go ahead and play!"?

Won't the blue sky wither
even beyond our death?
If it really doesn't wither,
if it doesn't,
why does it keep silent?
While we are living
why does the sky
grow dark all alone,
on the street, in a village, at sea?

(Translated by William I. Elliott & Kazuo Kawamura)

牧歌

陽のために
空のために
私は牧歌をうたいたい
人のために
土のために
私は牧歌をうたいたい
真昼のために
深夜のために
私は牧歌をうたいたい

名も知らぬ若木の下に立ちどまって
虻の羽音に耳をすまし
陽のささぬ露地の奥で
子供の立小便をみつめていたい

うたうため　うたうため
私はいつも黙っていたい
私は詩人でなくなりたい
私は世界に餓えているから

虻のように蝶のように
私は私の羽根でうたいたい
垢だらけの子供のように
私は私の小便でうたいたい

いつの日か
すべてを忘れるための牧歌を
私は私の死でうたいたい
丁度今日
すべてを憶えているために
私が本当は黙っているように

牧歌

为了太阳
为了天空
我想唱一支牧歌
为了人类
为了土地
我想唱一支牧歌
为了正午
为了深夜
我想唱一支牧歌

在不知名的小树下止步
倾听虻的振翅之声
在太阳照不到的小巷深处
我想凝视站着撒尿的孩子

为了歌唱　为了歌唱
我常常想沉默不语
我不想再成为诗人
因为我对世界正充满渴望

像虻和蝴蝶
我想用我的翅膀歌唱
像满身污垢的孩子
我想用我的小便歌唱

不知是哪一天
为了忘却全部的牧歌
我想用我的死亡歌唱
正像为了记忆一切
我真的像陷入了沉默的
今天一样

A Pastoral Song

I wish to sing a pastoral song
for the sunlight,
for the sky.
I wish to sing a pastoral song
for people,
for soil.
I wish to sing a pastoral song
for mid-day,
for midnight.

I wish to stand beneath a young tree of unknown name,
listen to a horsefly's buzzing
and watch a child peeing
way down an alley where there's no sunlight.

In order to sing, in order to sing
I wish always to keep silent.
I wish to stop being a poet,
for I am hungry for the world.

Like a horsefly, like a butterfly,
I wish to sing with my wings.
Like some grimy kid
I wish to sing with my pee.

Someday
I wish to sing with my death
a pastoral song to forget everything;
just as today,
I keep silent, really,
so that I can remember everything.

(Translated by William I. Elliott & Kazuo Kawamura)

海

雲のつむじの下
波立つ星の皮膚

時に巨大なタンカーを
小枝のようにへし折り

時に小さな丸木舟を
やさしく漂わせ

未だ現像されてない
陸の陰画

紋様を紋様にむすび
神と神をへだて
島々を閉じこめ
奴隷を運び

輝く白へと砕ける
最も重い青

貧しい漁夫には
網いっぱいの魚

夢見る少年には
ひとすじの水平線

彼岸へとくり返す
未生以前のどよめき

海よ

大海

在翻卷的云下
浪花涌动着星星的皮肤

有时，巨大的油轮
会像树枝一样被折断

有时，又使独木舟
优雅地漂浮

是一张未被冲洗的
陆地的底片

浪波连接着浪波
隔开神与神
将无数的岛屿关起来
贩运奴隶

粉碎着闪烁的白浪
是最最深沉的碧蓝

对于贫穷的渔夫
是满满一网捕捞的鱼

对于做梦的少年
一道地平线

向着彼岸反复拍打
是人类诞生前的声响

大海哟!

The Sea

Under a whirlpool of clouds,
the skin of our wave-washed planet…

Sometimes a mammoth tanker is snapped
like a tiny twig.

Sometimes it gently cradles
a dugout canoe.

It is an undeveloped
negative of land.

It joins pattern to pattern;
it separates god from god.
It encloses islands
and transports slaves.

The heaviest blue breaks
into radiant white.

A netful of fish
for a poor fisherman.

A streak of horizon
for a dreaming boy.

The roaring that precedes life
roaring towards the after-life.

Ah, the sea!

(Translated by William I. Elliott & Kazuo Kawamura)

色の息遣い

色

色はとどまることがない、ある色は他の色の予感、そして思い出、ある色は他の色をかくし、またあらわす、絶えず流れ、しりぞけあいながらまじりあい、色はたがいに演技しあい、変装しあう。色の息遣いを名づけることはできない、それらはいつか薄明へと褪せてゆくが、ふたたび恥じらいつつよみがえる、生あるものの歓びのために。

白

雪の白ではない、霜の白ではない、波の白ではない、雲の白ではない。塗られた白ではない、塗り残された白ではない、さらされた白ではない、けずられた白ではない。空白の白ではない、輝く白ではない、けがれなき白ではない、初まりの白でも、終りの白でもない。本当の白は何か。

黒

黒。それは中身をもたない。黒、それはどんな深みにおいてすら表面である。黒を照らし出す光は、黒に奪われる。黒は何ひとつ私たちに返してくれない。それはすべてを呑みこみ、みずからに同化する。

どんなに小さくとも、それは一個のピリオド、だがそれは汚点ではない。きわめて硬質で重いが、その特質を備えた物質は、いまだこの地上に発見されていない。私たちはただ時折の悪夢のうちにのみ、真正の黒の一端に触れることができる。黒。それは色ではなく、ひとつの在りかたである。

赤

赤は闇から立ち上る、赤はむしろ黒の庶子、だがその叫びを誰も聞きとることができない。赤は光へと死に絶える、赤はむしろ白のいけにえ、だがその願いはほんの束の間かなえられるだけ。

青

どんなに深く憧れ、どんなに強く求めても、青を手にすることはできない。すくえば海は淡く濁った塩水に変り、近づけば空はどこまでも透き通る。人魂もまた青く燃え上るのではなかったか。青は遠い色。
漠としてかすむ遠景へと歩み入り、形見として持ち帰ることのできるのは、おそらく一茎のわすれなぐさだけ、だがそれをみつめて人は、忘れてはならぬものすら忘れ果てる。おのがからだのうちにひそむ、とこしえの青ゆえに。

黄

黄。切り裂いて閃くもの、恥を知らずあらわにするもの、いつまでもつづく耐え難い喚き声、まばゆい汚物が溢れ出る、誰にも埋めることのできない世界の裂け目から。目はそこに吸い寄せられる、そして目はそこで拒まれる。あらゆる細部を失って、目は滑ってゆく、質感のない黄の、輝きわたる地平を、きりもなく。

緑

なにかしら異っているのだ、この緑という色は。別世界からもたらされたのだ、突然なんの前触れもなく押し入ってきたのだ、おそろしい生命に満ちて、むんむん匂い立っている。この星に初めて緑がはびこったとき、私たちは生まれていなかった。この星が緑におおいつくされるとき、私たちのすべては廃墟。緑から目を離すな。

茶

あるいは黄に、あるいは赤に、絶えず侵蝕されながらも、茶はその諧調のうちにへりくだる。かたくなな自信に支えられて、茶はすべてがやがて自分に還ってくることを夢見ている。茶はさりげなく世界をカモフラージュする、あたかも何ひとつ劇は起らないとでもいうかのように。それはたしかにひとつの賢い方法だ、宇宙の悪意から身を守るための。

颜色的气息

颜色

颜色不会停留，有的颜色是别的颜色的预感和回忆；有的颜色遮掩着别的颜色，或者表露和不断地漂流，互相拒绝着混杂在一起，颜色互相表演，互相乔装。颜色的气息无法命名，不知何时尽管它们渐渐地朝向黎明褪去，但是，又一次的羞怯继而苏醒，为了生的欢喜。

白色

不是雪的白色，不是霜的白色，也不是浪的白色，更不是云的白色。不是被涂上的白色，不是没被涂上的白色，不是被漂白的白色，也不是被刮掉的白色，更不是空白的白色。不是耀眼的白色，不是纯洁的白色，也不是最初的白色，更不是终结的白色。而真正的白色是什么？

黑色

黑色。它是空洞的。黑色，它在什么样的深度里都只是一个表面。照耀黑色的光，被黑色攫取。黑色不会把任何东西返还给我们。而且它吞噬全部，同化为己有。

无论怎样的渺小，它都是一个黑点，但不是污点。质地是极其坚硬和沉重的，但，具备它特质的物质，现在还没有在这片土地上发现。我们有时只是在噩梦里，能够触摸到真正黑色的一端。黑色，它不是颜色，它是一种存在状态。

红色

红色从黑暗中升起，红色宁愿是黑色的私生子，所以，谁也无法听见它的呼唤。红色朝向光死绝，红色宁愿是白色的供品，所以，那个愿望只是在短暂的一瞬如愿以偿。

蓝色

无论怎样深深的憧憬和强烈渴望，蓝色都不会搞到手。如果掬在手里，大海变成淡淡混浊的盐水，如果走近，天空通体透明。鬼火不是也在蓝蓝地燃烧着吗？蓝是遥远的颜色。

走进广袤云雾霭霭的远景，作为纪念品能带回到家里的，大概只会是一棵勿忘草，所以，发现它的人，连不能遗忘的事情都忘却了。蕴藏在自己的体内，因为是永恒的蓝色。

黄色

黄色。是劈开时闪烁的物质，是暴露了不知耻辱的物质，是总是难以忍受的呼唤声，是晃眼夺目污垢的溢出，是谁都无法填平的世界裂缝。

目光被吸引，然后在此又被拒绝。一切细节丧失，目光渐次滑行，没有质感的黄色、那灿烂广阔的大地是无边的。

绿色

总有点什么差异，这种绿色。它从别的世界带来，突然没有任何预兆地闯进来，充满可怕的生命力，热气蒸腾地散发味道。绿色最初蔓延到这颗星球时，我们还没有诞生。这颗星球被绿色严严覆盖时，我们的一切都是废墟，目光请不要从绿色转移。

茶色

在不断侵蚀黄色或是红色的同时，茶色在一种谐调中是谦逊的。被顽固的自信支撑着，茶色梦想着所有的一切不久都会回归自己。茶色若无其事地掩饰世界，仿佛什么戏剧性的事情也不会发生，这确实是一个高明的办法，为了在宇宙的恶意中守护住自己。

The Breaths of Colors

Colors

Colors never cease, one color being the prelude to another as well as its memory; one color hiding another even as it expresses it; flowing in mutual acceptance and rejection; switching roles and disguising one another. The breaths of colors are unnamable. Over time they fade into twilight, but they revive shyly for the joy of living things.

White

Not the white of snow, not of frost, not of waves, nor of clouds. Not a painted white, nor the white of an unfinished painting. Not a bleached white and not the planed-down white of wood. Not the white of the blank page, or shining white. Nor yet a pure white. Not the white of beginning or end. What is a true white?

Black

Black. It is without content. Black. However thick, it is a mere surface. Black steals the very light that illuminates it. Black returns nothing to us. It swallows everything and identifies what it swallows for itself alone.

Even a pinpoint, however tiny, is a period—not a stain.

Extremely hard and heavy. Yet no substance so far has been discovered on earth that is possessed of its characteristics. Only in a stray moment of a nightmare can we touch the edge of pure black. Black. It is not a color but a mode of being.

Red

Red emerges from darkness. It's rather a black's bastard, but its scream is inaudible. Red dies away into light, being rather a sacrifice offered to white. But its wishes can be heard only for a mere instant.

Blue

Regardless of how deeply we crave it and how intensely we desire it, we cannot obtain blue. Scooped up, the sea is merely pale muddy salt water. Approached, the sky is endlessly transparent. Doesn't a will-o'-the-wisp also burn blue? Blue is a far away color.

When we journey into the distant misty region, we can only bring back one single forget-me-not as a memento. People upon seeing this souvenir, however, forget what should not be forgotten because of the eternal blue hidden in their own inner depths.

Yellow

Yellow. It flashes when a thing is torn. It's something that unashamedly exposes itself, an intolerable and uninterrupted scream. Dazzling muck ceaselessly overflows out of the world's unfillable cracks.

Eyes are drawn by them and are rejected there. Having lost all details, eyes slide continuously along the shining horizon of the impalpable yellow.

Green

There is something unique about this color "green". It has been introduced from another world. It has intruded suddenly, with no warning whatever, filled with fearful life, and is odoriferous. When green first flourished on this planet we ourselves were not yet born. When green has at last encroached upon every inch of the earth, all we have and are will be ruins. Don't take your eyes off green.

Brown

Brown, always eaten at by yellow or red, is self-abased

into its own harmony. Propped up by obstinate self-confidence, it dreams of the time when all will come full circle back into brown. Brown nonchalantly camouflages the world, as if no drama will ever occur. This is clearly a ploy wisely designed to protect itself from the spite of the universe.

(Translated by William I. Elliott & Kazuo Kawamura)

海の比喩

人が海を見るのではない
海が人を見ているのだ
太古から変わらぬきらめく目差しで

人が海を聞くのではない
海が人を聞いているのだ
水底にひそむ無数の貝殻の耳で

ひとすじの水脈をひき人は旅立つ
消え去ることのない水平線をめざして
大時化と凪にもてあそばれながら

一組の箸と茶碗がいくつかの鍋が　そして
あふれ波立ちしたたり湛える感情が
女と男をむすぶだろう

だがそれらよりさらに深く強くふたりをむすぶもの
それは海というこの全いもの
飽くことなくくり返し尚美しいもの

人が海を歌うのではない
海が人を歌っているのだ
海が人を祝っているのだ

海的比喻

不是人看海
而是海看人
用亘古不变的炯炯眼神

不是人听海
而是海听人
用无数潜伏水底贝壳的耳朵

留下一条航迹，人启程
向着永不消失的地平线
任狂风怒潮和平静的水浪摆布

一副碗筷几口锅，然后
汹涌澎湃充盈欲滴的情感
将女人和男人联结

但是，还有比这更强烈的东西联结着两个人
那就是完整的大海
它不厌其烦地重复却依然美丽

不是人在歌唱海
而是海在歌唱
和祝福着人

The Metaphor of the Sea

Not that people look at the sea—
the sea with shining eyes looks at people,
eyes unchanged from the beginning of time.

Not that people hear the sea,
the sea hears people
with the ears of numberless shells under the seabed.

People set out on a journey towards an indelible horizon,
dragging a single seam of water,
and at the mercy of the storm and lull of the sea.

What will bring the man and woman together are
matched chopsticks and teacups, some pots and pans,
and emotions that bubble, boil and overflow.

What binds them even more profoundly, however, is
this wholeness called the sea,
the tirelessly repeating, ever beautiful sea.

Not that people sing of the sea—
the sea sings of people.
The sea celebrates people.

(Translated by William I. Elliott & Kazuo Kawamura)

頼み

裏返せ　俺を
俺の中の畠を耕せ
俺の中の井戸を干せ
裏返せ　俺を
俺の中身を洗ってみな
素敵な真珠が見つかるだろう

裏返せ　俺を
俺の中身は海なのか
夜なのか
遠い道なのか
ポリエチレンの袋なのか
裏返せ　俺を
俺の中に何が育っている
熟れすぎたサボテン畑か
一角獣の月足らずの赤坊か
ヴァイオリンになりそこなった栃の木か
裏返せ　俺を
俺の中身を風にさらせ
俺の夢に風邪をひかせろ
裏返せ　俺を
俺の観念を風化させろ

裏返せ
裏返してくれ　俺を
俺の皮膚を匿してくれ

俺の額は凍傷にかかっている
俺の眼は羞恥で真赤
俺の唇は接吻に飽きた
裏返せ
裏返してくれ俺を
俺の中身に太陽を拝ませてやってくれ
俺の胃や膵臓を草の上にひろげて
赤い暗闇を蒸発させろ
俺の肺臓に青空を詰めろ
俺の輸精管はもつれたままで
黒い種馬たちに踏みにじらせろ
俺の心臓と脳髄は白木の箸で
俺の恋人に食わせてやってくれ

裏返せ
裏返してくれ　俺を
俺の中の言葉たちを
喋らせちゃってくれ　早く

俺の中の弦楽四重奏を
鳴らしちゃってくれ
俺の中の年とった鳥たちを
飛ばしちゃってくれ
俺の中の愛を
すっちゃってくれ　悪い賭場で

裏返せ裏返してくれよ俺を
俺の中のうその真珠はくれてやるから
裏返してくれ裏返してくれよ俺を
俺の中の沈黙だけはそっとしといて
行かせてくれ俺を
俺の外へ
あの樹蔭へ
あの女の上へ
あの砂の中へ

恳求

把我翻过来
耕播我内心的田地
干涸我内心的井
把我翻过来
浣洗我的内心
也许会发现美丽的珍珠

把我翻过来
我的内心是海
是夜
是遥远的征途
还是聚乙烯塑料袋呢？
把我翻过来
我心灵的深处有什么正在发育
是仙人掌熟透的荒野吗？
是早产的独角兽的幼崽吗？
是未被制成小提琴的枥木吗？
把我翻过来
让风吹拂我的内心
让我的梦想感冒把我翻过来
让我的观念风化！

翻过来
把我翻过来
掩藏起我的皮肤
我的额头冻伤
我的眼睛因羞耻而充血
我的双唇厌倦了接吻
翻过来
把我翻过来！
让我的内心膜拜太阳
让我的胃和胰脏摊在草坪上
让紫血色的阴暗蒸发
把蓝天填入我的肺脏
任我的输精管扭结在一起
任黑色的种马踏烂成泥
将我的心脏和脑髓用白木筷子
喂给我的恋人吃

翻过来
把我翻过来！
把我内心的语言
吐出来！快！
让我内心的管弦乐四重奏

鸣响
让我内心的老鸟们
去飞翔！
把我内心的爱
在黑暗的赌场赌掉吧！

翻过来把我翻过来
我将内心谎言的珍珠给你
翻过来把我翻过来
不要去触摸我内心的沉默
让我走
走出我之外
向着那树荫
向着那女人身之上
向着那沙丘

Request

Turn me inside out
Plow the field inside of me
Dry up my inner well
Turn me inside out
Wash my insides
You might find a gorgeous pearl

Turn me inside out
Are my insides a sea
or night
or a distant road
or a plastic bag?
Turn me inside out
What's growing inside me?
An overgrown field of cacti?
Or a unicorn premie?
A horse chestnut tree that failed to become a violin?
Turn me inside out
Expose my innards to the wind
Let my dreams catch cold
Let weather wear away my ideas

Turn me inside out
For God's sake, turn me inside out
Hide my skin
My forehead is frostbitten
My eyes are red with shame
My lips are worn out from kissing
Turn me inside out
For God's sake, turn me inside out
Let my insides worship the sun
Spread my stomach and pancreas on the grass
and let the red darkness evaporate
Fill my lungs with blue sky
Let black stud horses
stomp on my tangled spermatic ducts
Let my heart and brain be plucked with plain chopsticks
and be eaten by my lover

Turn me inside out
For God's sake, turn me inside out
Let the words inside
be spoken, quickly
Let my inner string quartet

play
Let the aged birds within me
fly away
Let my inner love all be lost
in a crooked casino

Turn me inside out—C'mon, will you!
I'll give you the imitation pearls inside me
Please I beg you—Turn me inside out
but leave my inner silence alone
Let me go
out of myself
toward the tree shade of that tree
onto that woman
into that sand

(Translated by William I. Elliott & Kazuo Kawamura)

死んだ男の残したものは

死んだ男の残したものは
ひとりの妻とひとりの子ども
他には何も残さなかった
墓石ひとつ残さなかった

死んだ女の残したものは
しおれた花とひとりの子ども
他には何も残さなかった
着もの一枚残さなかった

死んだ子どもの残したものは
ねじれた脚と乾いた涙
他には何も残さなかった
思い出ひとつ残さなかった

死んだ兵士の残したものは
こわれた銃とゆがんだ地球
他には何も残せなかった
平和ひとつ残せなかった

死んだかれらの残したものは
生きてるわたし生きてるあなた
他には誰も残っていない
他には誰も残っていない

死んだ歴史の残したものは
輝く今日とまた来る明日
他には何も残っていない
他には何も残っていない

死去的男人遗留下的东西

死去的男人遗留下的东西
是妻子和一个孩子
其他什么也没被留下
一块墓地也没被留下

死去的女人遗留下的东西
是一朵枯萎的花和一个孩子
其他什么也没被留下
一件衣服也没被留下

死去的孩子遗留下的东西
是扭伤的脚和干掉的泪水
其他什么也没被留下
一个回忆也没被留下

死去的士兵遗留下的东西
是坏掉的枪和倾斜变形的地球
其他什么也没被留下
一个和平也没被留下

死去的他们遗留下的东西
是活着的我和你
别的谁也没曾留下
别的谁也没曾留下

死去的历史遗留下的东西
是辉煌的今天和将要到来的明天
其他什么也没曾留下
其他什么也没曾留下

What The Dead Man Left Behind

One wife and one child are
what the dead man left behind.
Nothing else—
not even a grave-marker.

One withered flower and one child are
what the dead woman left behind.
Nothing else—
not even clothing.

A twisted leg and dried tears are
what the dead child left behind.
Nothing else—
not even a memory.

A broken gun and a deformed Earth are
what the dead soldier left behind.
Nothing else—
not even any peace.

You and I the living are
what the dead left behind.
No one else remains.
No one else remains.

A shining today and another tomorrow are
what dead history left behind.
Nothing else remains.
Nothing else remains.

(Translated by William I. Elliott & Kazuo Kawamura)

灰についての私見

どんなに白い白も、ほんとうの白であったためしはない。一点の翳もない白の中に、目に見えぬ微小な黒がかくれていて、それは常に白の構造そのものである。白は黒を敵視せぬどころか、むしろ白は白ゆえに黒を生み、黒をはぐくむと理解される。存在のその瞬間から白はすでに黒へと生き始めているのだ。

だが黒への長い過程に、どれだけの灰の諧調を経過するとしても、白は全い黒に化するその瞬間まで白であることをやめはしない。たとえ白の属性とは考えられていないもの、たとえば影、たとえば鈍さ、たとえば光の吸収等によって冒されているとしても、白は灰の仮面のかげで輝いている。白の死ぬ時は一瞬だ。その一瞬に白は跡形もなく霧消し、全い黒が立ち現れる。

だが—

どんなに黒い黒も、ほんとうの黒であったためしはない。一点の輝きもない黒の中に目に見えぬ微少な白は遺伝子のようにかくれていて、それは常に黒の構造そのものである。存在のその瞬間から黒はすでに白へと生き始めている……

关于灰之我见

无论多么白的白，也不会有真正白的先例。在看似没有一点阴翳的白中，隐匿着肉眼看不见的微黑，通常，这就是白的结构。我们不妨这样理解，白非但不敌视黑，反而白正因其白才生出黑，孕育黑。从它存在的那一瞬间起，白就已经开始向黑而生了。

然而，在走向黑的漫长过程中，不论经过怎样的灰的协调，在抵达彻底变黑的瞬间之前，白都从未停止过坚守自己的白。即便白被影子、晦暗、弱光之类污染，白也一直在灰的假面背后发出光辉。白的死去只是一瞬。那一瞬，白消失得无影无踪，一种完整的黑顿现。然而——无论多么黑的黑，也不会有真正黑的先例。在看似没有一点光亮的黑中，隐匿着肉眼看不见的遗传因子一样的微白，通常，这就是黑的结构。从它存在的那一瞬间起，黑就已经开始向白而生了……

A Personal Opinion about Gray

There has never been a perfectly white white. Even in a perfect white an imperceptible trace of black is present and that is invariably the very nature of whiteness itself. White does not regard black as hostile; instead, white produces black because of its whiteness; white promotes black. From the very onset of whiteness, white points toward blackness. Whatever tones of gray it may undergo in its long journey toward black, white never ceases being white until the instant it turns into complete black. Even if white is violated by such non-white elements as shadow, dullness or absorption of light, white keeps shining behind a mask of gray. White dies in an instant. In that instant, white vanishes without a trace and complete black is born. But—
There has never been a perfectly black black. In a black that completely lacks radiance, an imperceptible trace of white is present, like a gene, and that is invariably the nature of blackness itself. From the very onset of blackness, black points toward whiteness.

(Translated by William I. Elliott & Kazuo Kawamura)

自己紹介

私は背の低い禿頭の老人です
もう半世紀以上のあいだ
名詞や動詞や助詞や形容詞や疑問符など
言葉どもに揉まれながら暮らしてきましたから
どちらかと言うと無言を好みます

私は工具類が嫌いではありません
また樹木が灌木も含めて大好きですが
それらの名称を覚えるのは苦手です
私は過去の日付にあまり関心がなく
権威というものに反感をもっています

斜視で乱視で老眼です
家には仏壇も神棚もありませんが
室内に直結の巨大な郵便受けがあります
私にとって睡眠は快楽の一種です
夢は見ても目覚めたときには忘れています

ここに述べていることはすべて事実ですが
こうして言葉にしてしまうとどこか嘘くさい
別居の子ども二人孫四人犬猫は飼っていません
夏はほとんどＴシャツで過ごします
私の書く言葉には値段がつくことがあります

自我介绍

我是一位矮个子的秃老头
在半个多世纪之间
与名词、动词、助词、形容词和问号等一起
磨练语言生活到了今天
说起来我还是喜欢沉默

我喜欢各种各样的工具
也喜欢树木和灌木丛
可是，我不善于记住它们的名称
我对过去的日子不感兴趣
对权威持有反感

我有着一双既斜视又有乱视的老花眼
家里虽没摆有佛龛和神龛
却有连接室内巨大的信箱
对于我，睡眠是一种快乐
梦即使做了，醒来时也全会忘光

写在这里的虽然都是事实
但这样写出来总觉得像在撒谎
我有两位分开居住的孩子和四个孙子但没养猫狗
夏天基本上是穿着 T 恤衫度过
我创作的语言有时也会标上价格

Self-introduction

I'm a short, baldheaded old man.
For over half-a-century
I've lived tossed about by words such as
nouns, verbs, postpositions, adjectives and question marks;
so I rather prefer silence.

I like tools;
and I very much like trees, as well as bushes,
but I'm not good at memorizing their names.
I'm not so interested in past dates
and I feel antipathy toward authority.

I'm squint-eyed, astigmatic and far-sighted.
I have no Buddhist altar or Shinto shelf-shrine in my house,
but I do have a huge mailbox that leads into my room.
I regard sleeping as a kind of pleasure
and though I have dreams I forget them when I waken.

What I'm describing here is factual
and yet I feel a false note is struck when things are put
into words.
I have two children living separately and four
grandchildren, and keep no dogs or cats.
I spend most of the summer in T-shirts.
The words I write are sometimes given prices.

(Translated by William I. Elliott & Kazuo Kawamura)

作者简介

谷川俊太郎，1931年生于东京，为著名哲学家谷川彻三的独生子，日本最负盛名的当代诗人之一。他高中毕业后，决定不再升学。于1952年出版首部个人诗集《20亿光年的孤独》，随后创作近70部诗作集，囊括日本各大文学奖，并从事散文、广播与电影剧本、儿童图书的创作。曾翻译《鹅妈妈童谣》，并长期担任《花生漫画》连载的翻译工作。曾在美国、爱尔兰、英国及中国朗诵诗作，其多部诗集被译为英文，如《20亿光年的孤独》（1996年英译版）、《62首十四行诗》（1975年原文版，1992年英译版）、《关于爱》（1995年原文版，2003年英译版）、《寂静伴我》（1968年原文版，1975年英译版）、《午夜厨房我只想与你倾谈》（1975年原文版，1980年英译版）、《定义》（1975年原文版，1992年英译版）、《可口可乐课程》（1980年原文版，1986年英译版）、《天天的地图》（1982年原文版，1996年英译版）、《忧郁顺流而下》（1988年原文版，1988年英译版）、《赤裸》（1988年原文版，1996年英译版）、《关于赠人以诗》（1991年原文版，2005年英译版）、《不谙世故》（1993年原文版，2004年英译版）及《极简》（2002年原文版，2002年英译版）。英文版《谷川俊太郎诗选》于1983年在美国出版，《谷川俊太郎：诗作选》于1998年在英国出版。近作《钟情》（SUKI）出版于2006年5月。

Shuntarō Tanikawa was born in 1931 in Tokyo. He is the only child of well-known philosopher Tetsuzō Tanikawa, and among the most popular contemporary poets in Japan. After finishing high-school, he decided not to go on to university. His first book of poems *Two Billion Light-Years of Solitude* appeared in 1952. He has since produced some 70 books of poetry and won every major Japanese award for his writings. He has also written essays, radio and film scripts and picture books for children. He is the translator of the *Mother Goose Rhymes* and has for many years been the translator of *Peanuts*. He has performed his poems in America, Ireland, England and China. His books of poems which have so far been translated into English are *Two Billion Light-Years of Solitude* (trans. 1996), *62 Sonnets* (1953, trans. 1992), *On Love* (1955, trans. 2003), *With Silence My Companion* (1968, trans. 1975), A*t Midnight in the Kitchen I Just Wanted to Talk to You* (1975, trans. 1980), *Definitions* (1975, trans. 1992), *Coca-Cola Lessons* (1980, trans. 1986), *Map of Days* (1982, trans. 1996), *Songs of Nonsense* (1985, trans. 1991), *Floating the River in Melancholy* (1988, trans. 1988), *Naked* (1988, trans. 1996), *On Giving People Poems* (1991, trans. 2005), *The Naif* (1993, trans. 2004) and *minimal* (2002, trans. 2002). *The Selected Poems of Shuntarō Tanikawa* was published in America in 1983 and *Shuntarō Tanikawa: Selected Poems* was published by Carcanet, U.K. in 1998. His most recent book of poems is *SUKI* (*Liking*), published in May 2006.

图书在版编目（CIP）数据

海的比喻：日汉英对照 / （日）谷川俊太郎著；田原译. -- 南京：江苏凤凰文艺出版社，2021.1

（红狐丛书. 一衣带水的相望）

ISBN 978-7-5594-1387-1

Ⅰ. ①海… Ⅱ. ①谷… ②田… Ⅲ. ①诗集－日本－现代－日、汉、英 Ⅳ. ①I313.25

中国版本图书馆CIP数据核字(2017)第272938号

红狐丛书·一衣带水的相望：海的比喻

北岛 主编
（日）谷川俊太郎 著
田原 译

出 版 人 张在健
责任编辑 王娱瑶 于奎潮
特约编辑 薛 倩 傅春晖
书籍设计 周伟伟
责任印制 刘 巍
出版发行 江苏凤凰文艺出版社
南京市中央路165号，邮编：210009
出版社网址 http://www.jswenyi.com
印 刷 苏州越洋印刷有限公司
开 本 880×1230毫米 1/32
印 张 3.125
字 数 33千字
版 次 2021年1月第1版
印 次 2021年1月第1次印刷
标准书号 ISBN 978-7-5594-1387-1
定 价 128.00元（全七册）

红狐丛书·东亚卷 | 北岛 主编

Poem in Blue

青の詩

蓝之诗

Noriko Mizuta

［日］水田宗子 著 田原 毛乙馨 译

江苏凤凰文艺出版社
JIANGSU PHOENIX LITERATURE AND ART PUBLISHING

目录

Contents

Poem in Blue

Noriko Mizuta

深い眠りがあったら

深い眠りがあったら
目覚めてくるものがあろうに
季節が移れば
野の草も蕾を付けてくるように

列車に乗っているならば
後ろにおいていくものものに
別れの一瞥をなげかければいい
河の土手に立ちすくんでいた男
踏切で手をつないでいた幼い兄弟

すべては一瞬の決別
後ろに過ぎ去って行くスピードは
わたしの脚では
取り戻しに走れない

微睡んでいるのは
深い円筒の中
まわりながら
滑りながら

どこまで行っても不十分な
落下
底なしの誘惑
奈落まで落ちる覚悟でも
辿り着けない
傷口へ
目覚めが頼りの
願望
微睡んでいるのは谺の中
無すら反復する深い幻の谷間
霧の中から
還り続ける
音無しの音
過ぎ去らぬ時のエコー

如若沉睡

如若沉睡
总有什么会来唤醒
正如时光荏苒
野草也会长出花蕾

如若搭乘列车
向车尾消逝的一切
投上离别的一瞥便已足够
河堤上呆立不动的男子
道口上牵着手的年幼的兄弟

一切都是一瞬间的诀别
向后退去的速度
我的双脚
无法追回

假寐
是在深深的圆筒中
绕啊绕
滑啊滑

到哪里都不满意
坠落
无底的诱惑
连一落到底的觉悟都
无法到达
向伤口
许下清醒藉以仰仗的
愿望
假寐是在回声中
连“无”都会反复的幻觉之深谷
从雾里
不断回归的无声之声
——无法成为过去的时间回声

If You Happen into a Deep Sleep

If you happen into a deep sleep,
An awakening will certainly follow,
Just as when the seasons change
And the field grasses put forth new buds

If you're riding on a train,
It's fine to send parting glances back
Toward all the things you leave behind
A man standing transfixed on a river embankment
Young siblings holding hands at a railway crossing

Everything is a momentary farewell
The speed of things disappearing behind,
I cannot reverse
Cannot run back to regain

Drifting off to sleep,
In a deep cylinder
Spinning away
Slipping away

Not enough, no matter how far it goes
Dropping
Bottomless temptation
Resolved to fall even to the underworld,
Never arriving
At the wound
Awakening's reliable
Aspiration
What is drifting to sleep amidst echoes
Reverberating nothing through the deep phantom valley
Out of the mist
Making its way home
Soundless sound
Never departing, echo of time

(Translated by Jordan A. Yamaji Smith)

詩は待っていてくれると

詩は待っていてくれると
T・S・エリオットは言った
魂は待っていてくれるだろうか
藪の中に潜んで
あるいは草原で寝転んで
わたしが追いつくのを
それとも
不意打ちをしてくれるだろうか
どこかで待ち伏せをして
辻斬りの腕でも試そうと

わたしも待っているのだろうか
こうして街を歩いていれば
あてどない放浪に似た
通過するばかりの
詩の中で
偶然出会うのではないか
向こうからこともなげに近づいてくる
見知らぬ国を通り過ぎていけば
突然背後から

呼び止められる
観光に訪れた
太古の廃墟で
地べたに座り込んでいるのではないか

わたしは見つめ続けてきた
爆発でできた宇宙が
ブラックホールに吸い込まれて
やがてすっかり消えてしまうように
わたしが記憶していた日々が
地の一点に吸い込まれていくのではと
それを見届けようと
この庭に舞い上がる
木の葉や灰塵に預けられた
魂のようなものが
徐々に
飛び散っていくのを

どこまで追っても
その先まで行き着けない

行く先定まらぬ旅路の物語を
どこかで語る詩人が現れるのを
詩はほんとうに
待っていてくれるのだろうか

如果诗会等待

T.S. 艾略特说过
如果诗会等待
那么，灵魂也会等我吧
藏于草丛
或卧躺草原
抑或
突然袭击
我的苦苦追寻
总之它潜伏在某处
等待着尝试武士手腕的初斩

我好像也在等待吧
如果这样走在街上
犹如毫无目的地流浪
在刚刚经过的
诗歌中
难道不是偶然遇见了吗？
从对面满不在乎地靠近
如果穿越未知的国度
突然从背后

被人叫住
在旅行到访过的
太古的废墟上
难道不是正席地而坐吗？

我不停地凝视
因爆炸而形成的宇宙
被黑洞吸入
很快消失殆尽
我记忆中的日子
也会被大地上的某一点吸
走为见证这一切
它们飘扬在这个庭院
被托付给树叶和灰尘
灵魂般的东西
慢慢地
飞散开去

无论追到哪里
也无法抵达终点

在某地讲述去处不明、旅途物语的
诗人现身之前
诗歌真的
会等待吗？

Poetry Will Wait for Me

Poetry will wait for me
T. S. Elliot wrote
I wonder if my soul will wait as well—
Lurking in the underbrush
Or sprawled on the field—
For me to come following
Or else
To greet me with surprise attack
Laying an ambush somewhere
Planning to test its new blade on my neck

Will I be waiting too?
Walking through town like this
Aimlessly, like a vagabond
In poetry
That just passes through,
Will we not end up meeting?
Careless approaching from over there
As I pass through this unknown country,
Leaping suddenly from the background

To challenge me
In these ancient ruins
Where I've come to sightsee
Here it is, sitting flat on bare earth

I have been staring at
This universe composed of explosion
As though inhaled by a black hole
Finally, disappearing,
These days I've held as memories
Inhaled into a single spot on the earth
Something like my spirit
Oversees as though to assure
That the leaves, ashes and dirt
Whirling up in this custodial garden
Gradually
Are scattered away

No matter how far it pursues
It can never arrive at the end

Where somewhere a poet will appear to tell
Tales from a road with unfixed destination
Will poetry really
Wait for that, I wonder?

(Translated by Jordan A. Yamaji Smith)

化石博物館にて

長い暗闇の中を上って来た
ゆっくりと時間をかけて
思えば
時間などあったのか
長いか短いか
自分だけ
といって
自分がわかってきたわけではない
樹か
石か
上へ上へ
少しずつ
頑なに
周りには
柔らかくなっていくものもの
下へ下へと
着実に
時を刻んでいる
気配
形を崩し
落ちてくるものを受け入れ

ああ　何というこの固さ
生き延びる
この冷たさ
吸収されない

ここに在り続ける
自分のまま
一〇〇億年
二〇〇億年
動かなかった
消えようともしなかった
溶けない軀
さようなら
暖かい湿り気
さようなら
醒めない眠り
遠いと近い
小さいと大きい
自分のまま
解けない意志

風の中で揺れた
光と雨をもとめて
手足を
のばせるだけのばした
夢の中の
意識の残影
周りに花々は咲いていたか
石のように
黙り
巨木のように
天を仰ぎ
一番乗りの孤独
その時
その小さい身体で
永遠を夢見
心を閉ざしたのか

気がつくと
見られている
ガラスの中の固いヒーロー

初めて花咲いた
晒しもの
意固地に生き残ろうと
石になった
あの美しさで
あの若さで
メドゥサに睨まれた
滅びゆく美から
朽ちない固さへ
そして
晒される栄光へ
電光のガラスケースの
灼熱のスポットライト
初犯の永久戦犯
最初に見つけられた功績
ガラスの中の永遠
それでも一〇〇億年がせいぜいの
瞬間の出来事
大きな建物の中の
一幕ものの舞台劇
初めて咲いた花の

ストーリー不明の物語
学者もわからぬ
シナリオライターはどこだ
遅れてやって来た
演出家
色のない
形だけ
身振りも台詞もない
寸劇の
なんという機嫌の良さ
なんという明るい舞台
なにもかも
封じ込めた
この感動

在化石博物馆

从漫长的黑暗中爬出
花时间慢慢
思考
时间真的存在过吗？
是长还是短？
虽说
孑然一身
却并不了解自己
是树木？
是石头？
向上、向上
一点一点地
变得顽固
周围全是
变软之物
向下、向下
踏实地
雕刻时光
迹象的
形状崩溃
接纳坠落之物

啊啊，这是何等的坚硬
这个幸存下来的
冰凉
不被吸收

厮守于此
按着自己的样子
一百亿年
两百亿年
一动不动
甚至从不打算消失
不融化的躯体
再见
温润的湿气
再见
不醒的沉睡
远和近
小和大
按着自己的样子
从不松懈的意志

摇曳于风中
希求光和雨
极尽所能
伸展四肢
梦中的
意识之残影
花朵在四周绽放了吗？
石头一样
沉默
如参天大树
仰望天空
最先抵达的孤独
那时
用它小小的身体
梦见永远
有过压抑吗？

缓过神来
被观赏的
玻璃里坚硬的英雄

第一次开了花
曾被唾弃
却坚挺地存活下来
变成石头
以那种美
和那种鲜活
与美杜莎对视
从走向灭亡的美
向着不朽的坚硬
而后
暴露于荣光之中
电光的玻璃罩里
灼热的聚光灯
初犯的永久战犯
最初被发现的功绩
玻璃罩里的永远
尽管如此，百亿年也不过
只是弹指一挥间
是雄伟建筑物里
舞台剧的一幕

初次绽放的花朵的
不明情节的故事
学者也不明白
编剧在哪儿
迟来的
表演者
无色
仅有形状
没有动作和台词
短剧
是多么快活
舞台又是多么明亮
一切都能
包容
此刻的感动

On the Fossil Museum

Rising through the long darkness
Slowly, taking its time
I reflect
Was there such thing as time?
So long, so brief
By myself
This
Isn't something I could come to understand
A tree?
A rock?
Upward, upward
Gradually
Obstinately
Through its surroundings
Substance that grows soft
Downward, downward
Steadily
Engraving time
Signs
Destroying shapes
Taking in things that come falling

Ah, how to describe this hardness
Long-living
This chill
That cannot be absorbed

Remaining here
Just as it is
Ten billion years
Twenty billion years
It did not move
Or disappear
Unmelting body
Goodbye
Warm moisture
Goodbye
Unwakening sleep
Far and near
Small and large
Just as it is
Unbreakable volition

It shook in the wind
Seeking sunshine and rain
Extended its limbs
As far as it could
Remnants of consciousness
In a dream
Did flowers bloom all around?
Like a rock
Staying silent
Like a giant tree
Revering the heavens
Leading the charge into solitude
That time
That small body
Did your heart close
Dreaming of forever?

Suddenly realizing,
It's being watched
Hero in hard glass

In first bloom
Bleached cotton
Obstinately trying to survive,
It became rock
With such beauty
Such youth,
Under Medusa's glare
From perishable beauty
To undecaying solidity
And
To refined glory
Lighted glass case
Incandescent stoplight
First offense of an immortal war criminal
First achievements discovered
Eternity in glass
Though at most, a ten-billion-year
Moment's worth of events
A one-act play performed
In a large building

First flowers to blossom
Epic of obscurity
Incomprehensible to scholars
Where are the screenwriters?
They've arrived so late
The directors
Colorless
Only with form
Without gestures or lines
This skit with
Such a fine mood
Such a bright stage
Anything, everything
Contained in
This action

(Translated by Jordan A. Yamaji Smith)

青の詩

記憶が薄れていく先は
青い空
野原に寝転んで行く先を追う
青が終わるところに昔があるのか
青が虚ろになるところは
白いナッシング
闇でないのがいい
空はすっぽりとあたりを包み
草原いっぱいの忘却
どこにも手がかりはない

わたしは
薄れた記憶を吸い込む
味のない
青

蓝之诗

记忆褪色的前方
是蓝天
横躺在草原去追赶那前方
蓝的尽头难道还有往昔？
在蓝成为空洞之际
只有白色的虚无
不是黑暗就已足够
天空覆盖周围
草原充满忘却
不论哪里都茫无头绪

我
吸入褪色的记忆
和无味的
蓝

Poem in Blue

Where memory goes fading on
Blue sky
Tumbling to the field, I follow
Where the blue ends, could long-ago be there?
Where blue goes blank
A white nothing
Better yet, a not-darkness
Sky envelops everything around
A meadow's worth of oblivion
Nowhere so much as a trace
I
Inhale that faded memory
Flavorless
Blue

(Translated by Jordan A. Yamaji Smith)

庭師——庭 1

今朝も男は庭を掃いている
竹箒を手に
落ち葉をかき集め
土にかすかな爪痕を残し
この囲みとられた小さな土地を
丁寧に浄めている

今朝も男は庭を掃いている
昨日も木の葉は散った
この庭に植えられ
この庭に休むことなく葉を落とす
樹々とともに
男は時を掃いていく
一夜のうちに過ぎて行ったものもの
はらはらと落ち
いつの間にかかき集められ
浄められていく
ものもの
男の竹箒は休むことはない
見て見ぬ振りをし
無関心にやり過ごし

やがて仕返しをされるのは
不意打ちであってほしいと
願うわたしは
庭師が頼りだ
庭師の腕がすべてだ
証拠を消し去り
跡形もなく
始末する
わたしの庭の僧侶
不浄な時に対面し
後始末をし続ける
職人技
囲っても囲っても
忍び込んでくる蔦のように
いつの間にか
庭の暗闇で待ち伏せているものを
朝にはかき集め
かすかな掃き目で整え
一日
見通しのよい

陽のあたる場所にする
庭の守番

春も夏も葉は落ち続け
秋も冬も葉は蘇り続ける
庭師の季節に終わりはない
黒衣の庭師
今朝も庭を掃いている

园艺师——庭院 1

今天早晨，男人又在打扫庭院
手持竹扫帚
将落叶扫到一起
地上留下些许的帚痕
在被圈起的一小片土地上
细心地扫除

今天早晨，男人又在打扫庭院
昨天树叶也落下
长在这庭院里的树
无休止地飘下落叶
与树木一起
男人打扫着时光
一夜间消失的东西
纷纷飘落
不知不觉被扫在一起
又被干干净净地
扫除净尽
男人的竹扫帚从不停歇
我却对他视而不见
甚至漠不关心

我祈祷他
以突然一击
给我最终的报复
园艺师才是依靠
园艺师的本领就是一切
销毁证据
踪迹全无
处理善后
我庭院中的僧侣
不洁时会出现
以匠人的绝技
继续清理
无论怎样围起院子
都像悄悄潜入的攀缘茎
不知不觉地
在早晨，将埋伏庭院暗处的东西
扫到一起
留下些许帚痕
一整天
眼界开阔

朝阳之处
充当庭院的守卫者

春夏之时亦有落叶不停
秋冬之际仍有枝叶复苏
园艺师的季节里没有终结
穿黑衣的园艺师
今天早晨又在打扫着庭院

The Gardener—Garden 1

This morning too, he is sweeping the garden
Bamboo broom in hand
Raking up the fallen leaves
Leaving faint scratches in the dirt
This tiny, enclosed plot of earth
He so carefully purifies

This morning too, he is sweeping the garden
Yesterday the leaves fell once more
Planted in this garden
This garden never rests, constantly shedding leaves
Along with the trees
He goes on sweeping time
This-and-thats which have come to pass in a single night
Fluttering down
Gathered up in a blink
Purifying these
This-and-thats
His bamboo broom never resting
Pretending not to see
Unselfconsciously working away

I want his eventual revenge
To be a surprise attack,
Praying this,
I depend on the gardener
The gardener's skill is all
Sweeping away the evidence
No vestige left
He finishes
Priest of my garden,
Facing up to time's defilements,
Continues to tidy up
Craftsmanship
Try as he might to preserve it,
Stealing in like ivy
In a blink
In the morning, gathering up
These things that ambush him in the garden's darkness
He handles with subtle sweeps
In one day
Creating a place with clear views

Where the sun shines
The garden's protector

Come spring, come summer, the leaves go on falling
Come autumn, come winter, the leaves go on rejuvenating
No end to the gardener's season
The gardener, in black clothes,
This morning too, he is sweeping the garden

(Translated by Jordan A. Yamaji Smith)

紫陽花——庭 6

梅雨前線に異常があって
紫陽花は青空の下で咲いている
照りつける日差しの中で
色を変える暇もなく
変身し遂げる余裕もなく
祭りをもりたてもしないで
一直線に満開

急がないで
急がないで
それでもあじさいは花
急いでも急がなくても
今年は終わり

紫阳花——庭院 6

梅雨前线发生了异常
紫阳花在晴空下绽放
毒晒的日光里
既无暇变色
也无力变身
更不为节日添色
一直盛开

不用急
不用急
即使如此，紫阳花依然是花
无论急还是不急
今年到此为止

Hydrangeas—Garden 6

Rather odd for the season of early summer rains
Hydrangeas, blooming under blue sky
Under the all-illuminating sunshine
No time for their color to deepen,
Too rushed for a full transformation
Without quite livening up the festival,
They burst into full blossom

Don't hurry
Don't hurry
But hydrangeas are after all a flower
Whether they hurry or not
This year will end

(Translated by Jordan A. Yamaji Smith)

〈くちなし〉の巻—佐川亜紀との四行連詩より

昨日は白かったのに　今日はもう土色
狡猾なくちなし
時の先回りをして
死をやり過ごそうとの変身術

⋆

メール送信にしっぱい
指と頭をつなぐ古びた回線のトラブル
しまい込んできたわたしの告白は
超特急で見知らぬひとへの落雷

栀子之卷——与佐川亚纪的四行连诗

昨天还是白的，今天却成土黄
狡猾的栀子
抢在时间之前
是意图逃避死亡的变身术

*

邮件发送失败
连接手指和大脑的老式线路出了问题
我一度深深隐藏的表白
如球状闪电飞快地落向陌生的地址

“Gardenias”—Verse from Four-line Renshi with Sagawa Aki

Though white yesterday today, already the color of dirt
Sly gardenias
Forestalling time itself
Trying to bypass death with their transformative craft
*
The attempt to send the email failed
Some trouble in that aged circuit between fingertip
and brain
My once deeply concealed confession
A lightning bolt Super-Expressed to unknown
addressees

(Translated by Jordan A. Yamaji Smith)

〈ガラス〉の巻―木島始との四行連詩より

ボストンは自殺した詩人たちの街
だが　この六月の日
街は一枚のガラスのように光り
どこにも記憶はない

⋆

落書きのようにとりとめのない
あなたからのＥメールのすべてを
６・８メガバイトの感度で保存する
いいかげんな心でメモリーはいっぱい

⋆

引越しのたびに燃やしてきたノートの束
旅に出ては忘れてきた他人のことば
舞いの彼方に消えていった蜉蝣の言の葉
ある日稲妻となって突然闇から還ってくる

玻璃之卷——与木岛始的四行连诗

波士顿是诗人自杀的城市
然而，在这六月的一天
城市好似一块发光的玻璃
哪里都不存在记忆
*
像乱涂乱画一样天马行空
你发送的电子邮件全部
以 6.8 兆的速度保存
马马虎虎的心里全是内存
*
搬家时烧毁的一捆捆笔记
出门旅行时忘掉别人的语言
飞向远方消失不见的蜉蝣之语
某一天变成闪电从黑暗中忽然出现

“Glass”—Verse from Four-line Renshi with Kijima Hajime

Boston, city of poets’ suicide

Yet this June day

The city shines like a single glass

Memory is nowhere

*

Your emails like endlessly scrawling graffiti

I always save them

In 6.8 megabyte sensitivity

My heart’s memory is full to brimming

*

Bundles of notebooks I’ve set ablaze whenever we moved

What set out on the journey were forgotten words

from some other

Words of a mayfly dancing off to vanish over yonder

One day, transformed into lightning, they come

zooming back from the darkness

(Translated by Jordan A. Yamaji Smith)

作者简介

水田宗子，著名诗人和女性主义批评家。水田宗子在东京女子大学文理学部毕业后，赴耶鲁大学留学并取得美国文学博士学位。先后在美国多所大学任教，1985年为创建城西国际大学回国，1992年创立城西国际大学。著有诗集《归路》《圣塔芭芭拉的暑假》《绿藻之海》等。评论集有《从女主人公到英雄——女性的自我与表现》《20世纪的女性表现——朝向性差异的外部》《语言纺织羽衣——女性的行旅物语》《现代主义思潮与“战后女性诗歌”的发展》《大庭美奈子的记忆文学》以及英文专著《埃德加·爱伦·坡的世界——罪与梦》《近代日本文学中的现实与虚构》等。水田宗子翻译有多部童话集和女性主义批评专著。她曾获得瑞典驻东京大使馆主办的马丁松国际诗歌奖，也被匈牙利政府授予共和国文化勋章，并获世界数十所大学颁授名誉博士和名誉教授，现为日本城西大学理事长。

Noriko Mizuta's free-verse poetry has blended transnational feminist perspectives with meditations on the meaning of family and home through five decades. Mizuta joined the Boomerang Society poetry circle when she was an undergraduate in Japan. She then continued writing in the U.S., publishing *End of Spring* (1976) and *Interlude* (1980), and co-authored *Amber in Flames* (1996) with Ohba Minako, while living in Riverside, California. Mizuta returned to Japan in 1985, and published her major critical works of modern Japanese women writers. She has established together with Chinese poets the Japan-China Association for Short Poetry. Mizuta has also translated works by Sylvia Plath, Anne Sexton, and E. Ann Kaplan into Japanese. In 2009, she founded the poetry journal *Carillon* Street. Recent collections have included *The Road Home* (2008); the three-part *Summer Holidays in Santa Barbara* (2010), *A Wedding in Amsterdam* (2013), *Sabbath in Tokyo* (2015), and *Sea of Blue Algae* (2013), which explores themes of the life-cycle, humans' origins and destinations, and the acceptance of mourning. Mizuta received the Cikada Prize (2013), founded to commemorate Swedish poet and Nobel laureate, Harry Martinson.

图书在版编目（CIP）数据

蓝之诗：日汉英对照 /（日）水田宗子著；田原，毛乙馨译. -- 南京：江苏凤凰文艺出版社，2021.1

（红狐丛书. 一衣带水的相望）

ISBN 978-7-5594-1387-1

Ⅰ. ①蓝… Ⅱ. ①水… ②田… ③毛… Ⅲ. ①诗集－日本－现代－日、汉、英 Ⅳ. ①I313.25

中国版本图书馆CIP数据核字(2017)第272935号

红狐丛书·一衣带水的相望：蓝之诗

北岛 主编

（日）水田宗子 著

田原 毛乙馨 译

出 版 人 张在健

责任编辑 王娱瑶 于奎潮

特约编辑 薛 倩 傅春晖

书籍设计 周伟伟

责任印制 刘 巍

出版发行 江苏凤凰文艺出版社

南京市中央路165号，邮编：210009

出版社网址 http://www.jswenyi.com

印 刷 苏州越洋印刷有限公司

开 本 880×1230毫米 1/32

印 张 2.75

字 数 26千字

版 次 2021年1月第1版

印 次 2021年1月第1次印刷

标准书号 ISBN 978-7-5594-1387-1

定 价 128.00元（全七册）

红狐
RED FOX

活字文化
Moveable Type

ISBN 978-7-5594-1387-1
9 787559 413871 >
定价：128.00元
（全七册）

红狐丛书·东亚卷 | 北岛 主编

我身体里的盐裙

The Salt Dress Inside Me

Kim Hyesoon

[韩] 金惠顺 著 薛舟 译

江苏凤凰文艺出版社
JIANGSU PHOENIX LITERATURE AND ART PUBLISHING

红狐丛书·东亚卷 | 北岛 主编

The Salt Dress Inside Me

我身体里的盐裙

내 안의 소금 원피스

Kim Hyesoon

［韩］金惠顺 著 薛舟 译

江苏凤凰文艺出版社
JIANGSU PHOENIX LITERATURE AND ART PUBLISHING

目录

Contents

The Salt Dress Inside Me

Kim Hyesoon

토성의 수면

나 눈 감으면 내 그림자들 다녀오는 곳
그곳에서 나는 연기로 만든 허리띠를 두르네
내 영혼이 저녁 모기떼처럼 앵앵거리면
그림자들 초원의 사자떼처럼 우글거리고
오늘 나를 태우고 남은 재가 일어나 춤추는 곳

토성의 달은60 개
그리하여 내 그림자는60 개
물론 눈동자는120 개
해가 뜨는지 마는지
눈을 다 떠보지도 못하네

그리하여 내 몸이 몇 개인지
몇 개가 더 죽을 수 있는지
땅은 물렁물렁하고 발걸음은 건들건들하고
공기는 끈적끈적하고 가슴은 우글우글하고
당신의 유령이 거미줄처럼 내 영혼을 채가는 곳

내가 나에게 명복을 빕니다
나는 죽은 몸들을 타고 앉아
남은 몸 몇 개를 재워보네
그리움도 자고 의심도 자고
아직 열지 못한 목구멍도 자고 다 잠들라

너는 죽어서 무엇이 되고 싶니?
나는 죽어서 테두리 없는 것이 될 거야!

계속해서 계속해서 달이 떠오르는 곳
두꺼운 이불로 내리눌러도
이빨이 삐죽삐죽 새어나오는 곳
가느다란 지평선에 거무튀튀한 사자들 걸터앉아
삐져나오는 야광 눈빛 자꾸만 자꾸만 감기는 곳
그곳의 그림자들과 다 이별하면 이곳의 내 몸무게
　　와도 다 이별하겠네

土星的安眠药

闭上眼，那是影子们去过的地方
我在那儿系着烟雾织成的腰带
如果我的灵魂嗡嗡像傍晚的蚊群
影子们开始蠕动，像草原的狮群
今天，我燃烧过的灰烬翩翩起舞

土星有六十颗月亮
所以我有六十个影子
当然就有一百二十只瞳孔
无论太阳是否升起
我都不能完全睁开眼睛

所以我有几个身体
几个身体可以死
大地绵绵软软，脚步摇摇晃晃
空气黏黏糊糊，心脏咕嘟咕嘟
你的幽灵像蛛网抓走我的灵魂

我为自己祈祷冥福
我坐在死去的身体上
哄睡剩下的几个身体
思念睡了，怀疑睡了
从未敞开的喉咙也睡了，都睡吧

你死以后想要变成什么？
我死以后渴望变得无边无际！

月亮不停地不停地升起的地方
蒙着厚厚的被子
牙齿还在尖锐冒出的地方
黑黢黢的狮子们蹲坐在修长的地平线
总是不停地不停地关闭夜光闪烁的眼睛
如果告别那个地方的影子
还要告别我在这个地方的体重

Saturn's Sleeping Pill

A place where my shadows visit when I close my eyes
There, I put on a belt made of smoke
When my soul buzzes like the mosquitoes at night
my shadows swarm like a pride of lions on the plains
A place where my ashes get up and dance after I've been
burnt today

Saturn has 60 moons
therefore, I have 60 shadows
I have 120 eyes, of course
I don't get to open all of my eyes
whether the sun rises or not

Therefore, how many bodies do I have?
How many more bodies can die?
The ground is soft-soft and my footsteps are limp-limp
The air is sticky-sticky and my heart heaves-heaves
A place where your ghost snatches my soul away like a
spider web

I pray for my own soul
I sit on my dead bodies
and put to sleep a few remaining live bodies
Longings are asleep doubts are asleep
even the throats that have not yet opened are asleep
        all asleep

What do you want to be when you die?
I'm going to be something that has no borders

A place where the moons rise continuously continuously
A place where teeth poke-poke out
even if you press them down with a thick blanket
A place where the dark sooty lions perch on the faint horizon
their eyelids keep keep falling on the glowing rays from their eyes
When you part with the shadows there
you also part with the weight of my body here

(Translated by Don Mee Choi)

전세계의 쓰레기여 단결하라

당신이 떠난 자리에 맥주병 두개 담배꽁초 한 개
　메모지 두장. 왜 내 전화를 먹니? 메시지를
　먹니? 먹을 게 그렇게 없니?
당신은 통신 부르주아. 나는 왜 항상 전화가 무
　섭니?
나는 당신이 쳐다보면 항상 무엇으로 변해야 할
　것 같아. 소파에 고꾸라진 옷 뭉치로 변하는
　건 어떨까?
아니면 뒤집어져서 버둥거리는
모든 짐승의 불쌍한 배처럼 얇다란 분홍색
누군가의 입술에 매달린 풍선껌은 어떨까?
당신은 아니? 눈동자의배꼽신. 팔뚝의귓바퀴신.
고구마무릎의사과씨신. 돼지발톱의병아리신.
꿈꾸는물방개의물푸레나무신.
어여쁜아가씨의뒤꿈치발톱신.
개미귀신의고양이눈깔신.
쥐구멍의고양이몸뚱아리추깃물신.
총체흔드는아줌마팔뚝의코끼리신.
프레온가스처럼터져나오는침방울
사자의썩은입냄새보다더굴욕구역질침샘신.

당신은 당신과 나의 사지에 매달린 신님들
모두 아니?
당신이 떠난 자리에 젖어버린 수건 뱉어버린 껌 뭉개진 토마토. 저마다 몽땅 몸을 빌어준 고마우신 검은 비닐봉지님들. 내 발 아래 콘크리트와 철근과 유리창의 깍지 낀 팔뚝들이여.
그 팔뚝들을 집요하게 내리치는 기계해머팔뚝들이여 드높아라.
전세계의 돼지여 단결하라 신. 전세계의 고양이여
버터가 되자 신. 손목들이여 팔뚝을 탈출하라 신.
축구선수 입에서 튀어나오는 욕설 무더기 고등어 시체 신. 인도에는 신님들 수가 3억. 사람은 거기 모두 몇 명 살까?
하늘 땅 바다에서 몰려온 별의 별 신님들.
당신이 떠난 자리에 내가 마치 쓰레기 신처럼 좌정하고, 사람에 대한 공복으로 이제껏 버티고 계신
저 더럽게 제일 높으신 신님처럼
쓰레기 매립지로 가는 초록색 트럭을
기다리고 있다는 거, 아니? 모르니?

매일 매일 빠져버린 당신과 나의 머리카락들이
저 멀리 바다에서 빙산 녹은 물과 섞이고 있다는
거, 아니? 모르니? 당신콧구멍의콧털따가운
지구한방울신!

全世界的垃圾，集合起来！

你离去的位置留着两个啤酒瓶、一个烟蒂、两张便条
为什么吞了我的电话？又吞了我的短信？这么饥不择食？
你是通讯资本家。我为什么经常害怕电话？
你盯着我看，我总感觉应该变成什么什么
变成倒在沙发上的衣服团怎么样？
还是像被翻过来苦苦挣扎的
野兽可怜的肚子，变成挂在某人
薄薄红唇上的泡泡糖？
你知道吗？
眼珠的肚脐神。胳膊肘的耳环神。
红薯膝盖的苹果籽神。猪脚指甲的雏鸡神。
做梦龙虱的花曲柳神。漂亮姑娘的脚后跟脚指甲神。
狮蚁的猫眼窝神。耗子洞的猫尸水神。
摇着鸡毛掸子的大婶胳膊肘的大象神。
像氟利昂那样迸出的唾沫星子。
比死者的腐朽口气更屈辱的恶心唾液腺神。

那些隐身于你我照片里的神，你都知道吗？
你离去的位置留着湿透的毛巾，吐出的口香糖，腐烂的西红柿。
每个慷慨出借身体的黑色塑料袋都值得感激。
我的脚下是混凝土和钢筋和玻璃窗的双手交叉的胳膊肘们。
顽固地锤打那些胳膊肘的机器锤胳膊肘们，抬高点儿。
全世界的猪啊，聚集起来神。全世界的猫啊
变成奶油吧神。手腕啊，逃离胳膊肘吧神。
足球选手嘴里迸出的脏话堆青花鱼尸体神。
印度神灵的数量是三亿。那里总共住着多少人？
天和地和大海里涌出的各式各样的神。
你离去的位置端坐着我，像垃圾神。
就像凭借对人的征服支撑到现在
最肮脏最崇高的神
正在等待开往垃圾填埋场的绿卡车，
你知道吗？不知道吗？

你和我每天都在脱落的头发

正与远处大海里冰山融化后的水相互混合，你知道吗？

不知道吗？

你鼻孔里的鼻毛，一滴滚烫的地球神！

All the Garbage of the World, Unite!

On the seat you left, two beer bottles, a cigarette butt,
two pieces of scratch paper.
Why are you screening my calls, my messages?
Don't you have anything else to do?
You are the bourgeoisie of communication. Why am I always
so afraid of the phone?
When you look at me, I always feel as if I should change
into something else.
How about changing myself into a pile of clothes
dumped on the sofa
or a pale pink wad of bubble gum dangling from someone's lips
like the poor tummies of all the animals that flail about when
they are turned over?
Do you know?
Eyesnavelgod. Forearmsearflapgod.
Sweetpotatokneesappleseedgod. Pigstoenailschickgod.
Dreamingdivingbeetlesashtreegod.
Lovelygirlsheelstoenailgod.
Antsghostscatseyeballgod. Ratholescatsrottingwatergod.
Mrsdustingarmselephantgod.
Salivadropexplodeslikefreongas.
Salivafountainevenmoremortifyingnauseatingthanthesmellofli

onsrottenbreathgod.
Do you know all the dearest gods that are hanging onto our limbs?
On the seat you left, a wet towel, a wad of gum, a crushed tomato.
Dear blackgarbagebags who thankfully lent each one of
their bodies.
Dear foldedarms of the window and concrete and steel
under my feet.
How high the armsofthemachinehammers that beat down
steadily upon those foldedarms.
All the pigs of the world unite god. All the cats of the world
let's become a butter god.
Dear wrists escape from the arms god. Heap of curses,
mackerel corpses spit out from a soccer player's mouth god.
There are 300 million gods in India. How many people live
there?
Dearest multiple gods that have swarmed in from the sky,
land, sea.
On the seat you left, I sit like a garbage god, and do you or
don't you know
that I wait for the green truck heading to the landfill like the
dearest dirtiest loftiest god
that has survived till now because of its hunger for humans?

Do you or don't you know that every day our hair falls and

mixes with the melting water of an iceberg in the faraway sea?

Yournostrilssingledropofapricklynosehairearthgod!

(Translated by Don Mee Choi)

인플루엔자

새라고 발음하면
내 몸에서 바람만 남고
물도 불도 흙도 다 사라지는 듯
그 이름 새는 새라는 이름의 질병인가
새는 종유석 같던 내 뼈에서 바람 소리가 나게 한다

날지 못하는 새들은 다 죽이라는 명령이 떨어졌다
죽일 새도 없으니 산 채로 자루에 넣어
구덩이에 파묻으라는 명령이 떨어졌다

나 시집와서 며칠 후 도마 위에 병아리를 올리고
그 털 벗은 것에 칼을 들어 내리치려할 때
갓 낳은 아기의 다리를 잡고 있던 기분
그 소름 돋은 것이 바들바들 떠는 것 같아
강보에 싸서 안아주고 싶었다

제 가슴을 베개 삼아 머릴 드리우고 잠들던 그것

정말 우리는 끝에 다 온 걸까?
악몽의 막이 찢기자 그 속에서 죽음이 탄생하고
　있다

내 심장이 한 마리 바람처럼 박자 맞춰 떤다

우리 마을엔 이제 날개 달린 것이 없다
다 땅 속에 넣고 소독약을 뿌렸다
큰엄마는 기르던 거위를 포대기에 싸서
들쳐 업으려다 방독면에 들켰다

내가 지금 새의 시를 쓰는 것은
새를 앓는다는 것
쇄골 위에 새 한 마리 올려놓고
부리로 쪼이고 있다는 것
사람이 죽으면 바람에 드는 것이라는데
나는 시방 새의 바람 속으로 든다

우리나라 하늘 연(鳶) 실이 다 엉켜
하늘 높이 쌓인 듯

흰 깃털 산이 바람에 힐끗거리고
그 속에 3 개월짜리 6 개월짜리 조그만 눈알들이
첩첩이 쌓여 있다
구덩이에 쏟아져 들어가기 몇 시간 전
눈 뜨고 떨고 있다

流感

当我说出“鸟”
身体里仿佛只剩下风
水、火、土都消失了
莫非鸟是一种名字叫鸟的疾病？
鸟让我钟乳石般的骨头发出风声

我们受命杀死所有不会飞翔的鸟
因为来不及，命令又说装进麻袋
活埋在土坑

出嫁几天后，我把小鸡放在菜板上
举刀砍向被拔光毛的小东西
仿佛我抓着新生儿的腿
长满鸡皮疙瘩的它在颤抖
我想把它包进襁褓，抱在怀里

那小东西枕着自己的胸膛打瞌睡

难道我们真的走到了绝境？
噩梦的膜被撕裂，死亡诞生

我的心脏像一缕风，跟着节拍颤抖

现在我们村里没有长翅膀的东西
它们都被塞进泥土，洒上消毒液
伯母用襁褓包起家养的鹅
背在身上，却被防毒面具揭穿

现在我正写一首鸟的诗
这意味着鸟让我疼痛
意味着一只鸟栖息在我的锁骨
啄我
他们说人死了会随风而逝
可是我刚刚走进鸟的风

仿佛国家的风筝线相互纠缠
高高地堆满天空

白色的羽毛山在风中窥视
那里层层叠叠
堆积着三个月、六个月的眼珠
落坑前的几个小时
它们还睁着眼睛轻轻颤抖

Influenza

When I pronounce “bird”
only the wind remains in me
as if water, fire, earth all vanish
Maybe the name “bird” is the illness of the name “bird”
The bird makes the sound of blowing wind from my
dripstone-like bones

We received an order to kill all the birds that couldn't fly
Since there was no time to kill, we received an order to put
them in a sack
and bury them alive in a pit

A few days after I got married I placed a chick on a
cutting board
and was about to strike the plucked bird with a knife
It felt as if I were holding the legs of a just-born infant
the chick covered in goose bumps was trembling
I wanted to wrap the bird in a baby's quilt and hold it in my arms

That thing that snoozes with its head pillowed on its chest

Have we really reached the end?
The nightmare's curtain rips and Death is born inside

Like a wall of wind my heart trembles to the rhythm

In my village now there are no such things with wings
on them
They have all been put in the ground, powdered
with disinfectant
My aunt was caught by Mr. Gas Mask
when she tried to wrap her goose in a baby blanket onto her back

The fact that I'm writing a bird poem means
that I'm ill with the bird
A bird perched on my collarbone
pecks me
They say when you die you go with the wind
but now I go with the wind of the bird

As if all the kite strings of my country have tangled and
piled up high in the sky

the white-feathered mountain flutters in the wind
and inside it 3-month old, 6-month old tiny eyes
heaped in layers
a few hours before they are shoved into the pit
they tremble with their eyes opened

(Translated by Don Mee Choi)

정작 정작에

정작 꽃집에는 없는 것, 흙
정작 새집에는 없는 것, 하늘
정작 물고기집에는 없는 것, 바다

우리집에 없는 것은 당신이 더 잘 알겠지?

쥐와 벼룩과 바퀴벌레를 힘껏 밀어내고
엎드려서 웅얼웅얼 글씨 읊조리고 있는 우리집
잡초와 빗줄기와 유령의 머리칼을 밀어내고
바람에 움찔움찔 계단을 터는 우리집

높은 집이라는 말 속에는 무엇이 들어 있나
추락한 인부의 이빨이 들어 있네
먼 집이라는 말 속에는 무엇이 들어 있나
담벼락에 붙은 늙은 엄마의 손바닥이 들어 있네

즐거운 집이라는 말 속에는 무엇이 들어 있나
소름끼치도록 말랑말랑해 두 주먹을 꽉 쥐지도
　　못하는
시시로 치미는 악령의 눈동자가 한 벌 들어 있네

하나님의 집에는 태어나라 죽어라 동사님들만 살고
우리 집에는 나 나 나 나 인칭대명사님들만 살고
자연의 집에는 무서워 무서워 무서워 형용사님들
만 살고

검은 샘 깊은 집엔 누가 누가 사나
땅 속에서 뱀처럼 깨어난 수맥이 살지

어느 날 장황한 소설이 지리멸렬하게 끝나듯
식구들 지상에서 모두 떠나고
꽃이 피고
나비 날고
저녁 가고
봄 오고
식사 같이 하실래요
영원히 죽지않는 시계에 사는 망치가 시간 맞춰
때려주는 집
이생에 태어나 몇몇 집에 살다 가게 되는지 헤아
리다가 잊어버렸네
이다음에 귀신이 되었을 때 나는
그 어느 집에 제일 자주 출몰하게 될까?

꿈밖에서는 알아들었는데 꿈속에서는
정작 못 알아듣는 말, 우리집
모여 살 때는 알아들었는데 정작 정작에
나 죽은 다음에는 못 알아듣는 말, 우리집
다음 생에선 엄마아빠오빠동생 우리 우리 어떻게
알아볼까?

그러나 그러나 배 가라앉고
바다속으로 잠겨 가면서도 눈 감지 못하던 눈동
자들!

집에 가고 싶어! 하던 눈동자들

真的，真的

真的，花店里没有的，是泥土
真的，鸟巢里没有的，是天空
真的，鱼缸里没有的，是海洋

我们家里没有什么，你是否应该更清楚？

我们家努力赶走老鼠、跳蚤和蟑螂
趴在地上嘟嘟哝哝地吟诵
我们家赶走杂草、雨点和幽灵的头发
颤悠悠地在风中清扫楼梯

高处的家，这个词里有什么有坠落工人的牙齿
远方的家，这个词里有什么有紧贴围墙的老母亲的手掌

欢乐的家，这个词里有什么有一双闪烁的魔鬼的眼睛
惊人地柔软，让你无法握紧拳头

上帝家里只住着动词先生——出生、死亡
我们家里只住着人称代词先生——我、我、我、我
自然的家里住着形容词先生——恐怖、恐怖、恐怖

谁，谁住在黑泉深处的家里？
像蛇一样从地下醒来的水脉

像冗长的小说支离破碎地结束
有一天，家人们全部离开大地
鲜花盛开
蝴蝶飞舞
夜晚过去
春天到来
一起吃饭好吗？
永远不死的钟表里摆锤按时敲响的家
细数此生住过的家，然后忘记
当我变成鬼魂
我会经常出没于哪个家？

我们家——梦境之外听懂的话
梦里真的听不懂
我们家——一起生活的时候听懂的话
却在死后听不懂
妈妈爸爸哥哥妹妹，我们，我们来生怎么相认？

可是，可是，船沉了
沉入大海，那些依然不肯瞑目的瞳孔！

那些呼喊“我要回家”的瞳孔

Really Really

Soil—the thing that's not at the flowerhouse, really
Sky—the thing that's not at the birdhouse, really
Ocean—the thing that's not at the fishhouse, really

You know better than I do the thing that's not at my house,
        right?

My house shoves out rats, lice, and roaches
prostrates and mutters-mutters reciting something
My house shoves out weed, rain, and ghost's hair
flinches-flinches from the wind, ripping the stairs

What's inside the words—A tall house?
The teeth of the fallen worker are inside it
What's inside the words—A faraway house?
My aged mommy's palms stuck to the wall are inside it

What's inside the words—A happy house?
The flashing demon's eyes are inside it
so terrifyingly soft that you can't make a fist

In God's house only Mr. Verbs—live, die—live in it
In my house only Mr. Pronouns—me, me, me, me—live in it
In nature's house only Mr. Adjectives—scary, scary—live in it

Who, who lives in the house with a deep dark spring?
The streaming groundwater awake like a snake lives in it

One day like when a lengthy novel ends incoherently
my family leaves this world and
flowers bloom
butterflies fly
night passes
spring arrives
Would you like to eat with me?
The house where the hammer lives inside the clock that
never dies hammers on time
I wonder how many houses I get to live in during my
    lifetime, then I forget
Later when I become a ghost
which house will I appear in the most?

My house—the words that I understood outside my dream
but can't understand inside the dream, really
My house—the words that I understood when we
lived together
but can't understand after I'm dead, really, really
In my next life how would we, we mommydaddyolderbrothe
ryoungersister recognize each other?

However, however the boat sinks and
the sailors can't keep their eyes closed as they sink into the ocean!

Their eyes that said, "We want to go home!"

(Translated by Don Mee Choi)

하나님의 십자수와 레이스에 대한 강박 1

하나님의 십자수와 레이스에 대한 강박은
해가 뜨고 달이 뜨는 오래된 패턴북을 넘겨보면
알 수 있죠

가만히 안개 내리는 강가에 서 있어도 저절로 알
게 되죠

그 가늘고 투명한 실을 처음 손가락에 걸 때는
이토록 가벼워서 어쩌나 움찔하지만
긴 이야기 묘연한 레이스가 시작 되는 거죠
레이스는 자라서 피 묻은 속옷이 될까요?
강물에 떠내려가는 면사포가 될까요?
땅속에서 착용하는 복장이 될까요?

아 정말 신기한 무늬야 했지만
낡은 패턴북을 넘겨보면
엄마의 결혼 첫날밤 커튼처럼
그 무늬 속에 다 들어 있는 이야기

구멍 숭숭 뚫린 투명한 무늬들 속에
1월 1일　12월 18일　12월 25일

하나님은 십자수와 레이스 강박증 환자
커튼처럼 창틀에 걸터앉아 안팎의 비밀을 다 엿듣고는 펄럭 펄럭 하기만 하죠

나의 신경망이 엉킨 낚싯줄처럼 뭉쳐져선
난파선같이 출렁이는 바닥에 팽개쳐지는 날

빗금　빗금　빗금
물결　물결　물결

긁　긁　긁
금　금　금

크랙　크랙　크랙
스크래치　스크래치

하나님의 십자수와 레이스에 대한 강박은
산 채로 돼지 2천5백마리 파묻은 우리 큰집 앞 산자락을

흰 눈으로 몽땅 덮어놓은 걸 보면 금방 알 수 있죠

웅크리고 누운 죽음의 애벌레 속에서
희디흰 실을 물고 나비들 뿜어 나오듯

낡은 패턴북을 뚫고 점점이 날아오는 속눈썹과
속눈썹의 입맞춤 같은 흰 눈송이들

벌판 가득 가벼운 무늬가 눈 감고 숨 숨 숨 내려
　　오죠
소녀의 미소 같은 구멍들을 내뿜으면서

上帝对十字绣和蕾丝的痴迷 1

只要翻开日月升起的古老的样品书
你会知道上帝对十字绣和蕾丝的痴迷

即使安静地站在雾蒙蒙的河边也会知道

当你第一次在手上缠绕纤细而透明的线
那么轻盈，足以令你吃惊
其实漫长的故事开始于奇妙的蕾丝
蕾丝长大后会变成带血的内衣吗？
还是会变成漂在河水上的面纱？
还是会变成适合穿在地下的服装？

啊，多么神奇的花纹
如果继续翻看陈旧的样品书
像妈妈新婚之夜的窗帘
所有的故事都在花纹里隐藏

透明的花纹漏洞百出
1 月 1 日，12 月 18 日，12 月 25 日

上帝患上了十字绣和蕾丝的强迫症
偷听内外的秘密，像窗帘骑着窗框呼啦啦地响

那天我的神经网犹如交错的钓鱼线
像遇难的船只被扔进波涛汹涌的大海

斜线　　斜线　　斜线
波纹　　波纹　　波纹

划　　划　　划
裂　　裂　　裂

噼啪　　噼啪　　噼啪
沙沙　　沙沙

当你看见白雪覆盖着我家老屋门前
活埋了两千五百头猪的山麓

你会知道上帝对十字绣和蕾丝的痴迷

正如蝴蝶咬着雪白的丝线
涌出蜷缩成团的死亡幼虫

睫毛穿过陈旧的样品书点点飞来
而雪花白得就像睫毛的吻

轻盈的花纹闭上眼睛，落满旷野
喷涌而出的洞，犹如少女的微笑

God's Obsession Regarding Cross-Stitch and Lace 1

You can get to know God's obsession regarding cross-stitch
        and lace
by leafing through an old pattern book where sun rises
        moon rises

You can also get to know about it naturally as you stand still
by a riverside where mist is falling

When you wrap the thin and transparent thread around
your fingers for the first time, you may be startled,
        Goodness it's so light
but this is how the long story, the faint lace begins
Will the lace grow up to be a bloodied undergarment?
or a bridal veil floating away in the river?
or an outfit worn in the ground below?

Ah it's a really amazing pattern
but if you leaf through the worn-out pattern book
like the curtain of mommy's first wedding night
the story is all in the pattern

Inside the transparent patterns full of holes
January 1, December 18, December 25

God is a cross-stitch and lace obsessive-compulsive patient
He sits on the windowsill like a curtain and overhears all the
    secrets of the inside and out, flapping about

The day when my nervous system gets entangled like fishing lines
and thrown into the wavering bottom like a wrecked ship

slash slash slash
current current current

scrape scrape scrape
streak streak streak

crack crack crack
scratch scratch

You can get to know God's obsession regarding cross-stitch
    and lace

right away when you see that the foot of the mountain across
from my brother's house where 2500 pigs have
been buried alive is completely covered in snow

Like when the butterflies with the whitest threads in their
mouths spew out from the scrunched larvae of death

Eyelashes bore through the old pattern book and come
flying spot spot
the snowflakes as white as the kiss of the eyelashes

Weightless patterns close their eyes and fall on the field
breath breath breath
emitting holes like the smiles of a girl

(Translated by Don Mee Choi)

우가 울에게

11월에는 잠이 오지 않았고
11월에는 천장의 별이 모두 켜졌고
11월에는 가슴이 환해 눈을 감을 수 없었고
찬 우물이 머리보다 높아 쏟아질 듯 위태로웠고
우와 울은 주먹 쥐고 푸른 바게쓰 속에 누워
    있었네
충치 앓는 피아노처럼 둘이 앙다물고 있었네

우는 구름을 덮고, 울은 그림자를 덮었네
우는 바람에 시달리고, 울은 바다에 매달렸네
우는 살 냄새다 하고, 울은 물 냄새다 했네
우는 햇빛을 싫어하고, 울은 발이 찼네
우는 먹지 않고, 울은 마시지 않았네
밥을 먹는데도 내가 없고, 물을 마시는 데도 내가
    없었네

우는 산산이고, 울은 조각이고
우는 풍비이고, 울은 박산이고
내 살갗은 겨우 맞춰놓은 직소퍼즐처럼 금이 갔네
우는 옛날에 하고, 울은 간날에 울었네
우는 비누를 먹고, 울은 빨래가 되었네
나는 젖은 빨래 목도리를 토성처럼 둘렀네

우는 얼음의 혀를 가졌고, 울은 얼음의 눈알을 가
졌네
나는 얼음을 져 나르느라 어깨가 아팠네

왼쪽 어깨에 우를 오른쪽 어깨에 울을 물지게 가득
짊어진 여자가 나타났네
티베트 깡통 돌리는 할머니 염불처럼 천당 지옥
천당 지옥 계속 이진법이더니
우 다음에 울을 한 바께쓰 내 살갗 밑에 부었네
갔네

김수영은 김수영영영이고
김춘수는 김춘수수수이고
김종삼은 김종삼삼삼이고
왼발 다음엔 오른 발
0 다음엔 1, 2 다음엔 3 이고
우 다음엔 울이라고

세상에 가득 찬 수학이 출몰하는 밤
존경하는 시인님들은 아직 죽음의 탯줄에 매달려
계시고

콜리가 멜랑에게
12 월이 11 월에게

우는 빗줄기를 빗질하고, 울은 빗줄기를 빗질하고
우는 하얀 색 운동화를 왼쪽에 신고
울은 하얀색운동화를 오른쪽에 신고
나는 발잔등에 줄 끊어진 흰 새를 두 마리 덮고

그렇게 오도 가도 못했네

忧对郁说

11 月没有睡意
11 月天花板的星星都亮了
11 月心地通明我合不上眼
冰凉的井水高过头顶摇摇欲坠
忧和郁躺在蓝色的水桶里紧握着拳
它们沉默不语，像被虫蛀的钢琴

忧盖着云彩，郁盖着影子
忧忍受着风，郁纠缠着海
忧说肉香扑鼻，郁说清水无香
忧讨厌阳光，郁感觉脚冷
忧不吃饭，郁不喝水
当忧吃饭我不在，当郁喝水我不在

忧支离破碎，郁四分五裂
忧是风飞，郁是雹散
我皮肤皲裂像勉强拼起的七巧板
忧早已哭过，郁前天哭了
忧吃香皂，郁变成要洗的衣服
我像土星，围着湿漉漉的围巾

忧有冰的舌头，郁有冰的眼珠
我搬运寒冰，肩膀酸痛

一个女人走来，背架满满
忧在左肩，郁在右肩
天堂地狱天堂地狱，连续的二进制
像西藏的老奶奶转经念佛
先忧后郁的水桶在我皮肤底下肿胀又消失

金洙暎是金洙——000
金春秋是金春——###
金宗三是金宗——333[1]
左脚然后是右脚
0 之后是 1， 2 之后是 3
忧之后是郁

满世界数学出没的夜晚
尊敬的诗人们依然握着死亡的脐带

忧对郁说
12 月对 11 月说

忧为雨脚梳头，郁为雨脚耙地
忧把白色的球鞋穿在左脚
郁把白色的球鞋穿在右脚
我的脚背上盖着两只断线的白鸟

我就这样寸步难行

译注：

1 金洙暎、金春秋与金宗三都是韩国现代诗歌史上的著名诗人。

Dear Choly, From Melan

In November I was sleepless
In November the stars on the ceiling all lit up
In November my heart was so bright that I couldn't close my eyes
I was in a precarious state as the cold well rose above my head
Melan and Choly lay in a blue bucket, making fists
They clammed up like a cavity-ridden piano

Melan covered herself with a cloud, Choly with a shadow
Melan endured the wind, Choly clung to the sea
Melan said it's flesh-scented, Choly said it's water-scented
Melan disliked sunlight, Choly's feet were cold
Melan didn't eat, Choly didn't drink
I was absent when Melan ate, also when Choly drank water

Melan is a Frag, Choly is a Ment
Melan is a Dis, Choly is a Perse
My skin cracked like a jigsaw puzzle
Melan said long ago, Choly wept ages ago
Melan ate soap, Choly became laundry
I swirled the wet laundry around my neck like one of
    Saturn's rings

Melan has a tongue of ice, Choly has eyes of ice
My shoulders hurt from carrying ice

A woman appeared with a yoke loaded with
Melan on her left shoulder, Choly on her right
Heaven hell, heaven hell, continually binary
like a Tibetan grandma's spinning prayer wheels
The woman poured beneath my skin a bucketful of Melan
then Choly and left

Kim Su-yông is Kim Su-000
Kim Ch'un-su is Kim Ch'un-###
Kim Chong-sam is Kim Chong-333[1]
Step left then step right
After 0 is 1, after 2 is 3
After Melan is Choly

A night when all the mathematics of the world appear
The poets I admire are still clinging to death's
umbilical cord

Dear Melan, from Choly

Dear November, from December

Melan combed rain streaks, Choly plowed them

Melan put a white running shoe on her left foot

Choly put a white running shoe on her right foot

I covered up a pair of white birds, strings cut, on my feet

I couldn't come and go as such

(Translated by Don Mee Choi)

Translator's Note:

1 Kim Su-yông, Kim Ch'un-su, and Kim Chong-sam were prominent contemporary male Korean poets. The last syllables of their names "yông," "su," and "sam" are homonyms for numbers.

상처의 신발

상처에 발을 집어넣는다
상처를 신고 다닌다
아니면 상처가 냄새나는 발을 품고 다니는 건가
상처는 나를 위한 피고름 틀이다

상처로 지은 신발은 꽃 투성이
내가 발을 집어넣으면 진홍빛 피톨들이 짓이겨진다
상처로 지은 신발은 배를 가른 닭의 목구멍
내가 발을 집어넣으면 작은 갈비뼈들이 우두둑 부
　　러진다
상처로 지은 신발은 열린 무덤
내가 발을 집어넣으면 엄마 아빠 무덤 두 개가
내 왼발오른발에 신겨진다

상처의 신발은 가끔 발작하지만 대개는 참는다
물집이 터지고 썩은 냄새가 진동한다
진분홍 입술을 앙 다물고 내 더러운 두 발을 이빨
　　에 문다
신발이 아픈지 안아픈지 내 두 발은 모른다

상처의 신발은 방향 감각이 없다
늘 거기가 여기고 여기가 거기다
상처의 신발은 내가 발을 내딛는 곳마다 여기라고
　　주장한다
상처의 신발이 디딘 곳, 그곳이 내 잠깐의 영토다
신발이 커지면 발도 커진다
나는 뜨거운 쌀자루만큼 커진 신발을 신고
배갈라진 진 채 달아나는 흰 돼지처럼 뛰어오른다

상처로 지은 신발 속은 밥알 투성이다
내가 잘 지은 밥솥에 발을 집어넣는다
밥알들이 작은 생선 알들처럼 내 발밑에서 짓뭉개
　　진다
상처로 지은 신발은 엄마의 늘어진 가슴 두 쪽
　　이다
신발이 바닥에 닿으면 우유 같은 눈물 번진 흔적!
파리 떼 가득 붙은 뜨끈한 누군가의 목구멍 속으로
고린내나는 발가락을 집어넣는 이 감촉!

나는 지금 바깥쪽으로 약간 기울어진
상처투성이를 신고 땡볕 속을 걸어가고 있다

伤口的鞋子

脚伸进伤口
穿着伤口走
或者伤口抱着发出异味的脚？
伤口是为我而生的脓血模型

伤口做成的鞋子开满鲜花
我伸进脚，鲜花被碾成深红色的血珠
伤口做成的鞋子是破膛鸡的喉咙
我伸进脚，小小的肋骨嘎吱破裂
伤口做成的鞋子是开放的坟墓
我伸进脚，爸爸妈妈的两座坟墓
穿在我的左脚和右脚

伤口的鞋子偶尔发作，通常还是会忍耐
水泡破裂，腐烂的气味在荡漾
紧闭深粉色的唇，用牙咬住肮脏的双脚
鞋子是否疼痛，我的双脚不得而知

伤口的鞋子没有方向感
总把那里当成这里，把这里当成那里
伤口的鞋子认为我涉足的每个地方都是这里
伤口的鞋子走过的地方，那是我临时的领土
鞋子大了，脚也变大
我穿着像热米袋般越来越大的鞋子
跃起，像被剖腹之后逃跑的白猪

伤口的鞋子里盛满饭粒
我把脚伸进煮熟的饭锅
饭粒像小小的鱼子在我脚下被碾碎
伤口做成的鞋子是妈妈下垂的双乳
鞋子碰到地面，留下牛奶般的泪痕！
感觉像把腥臭的脚趾伸进谁的喉咙
苍蝇成群、滚烫的喉咙！

现在，我穿着稍稍向外倾斜的伤口
走向烈日

Wound's Shoes

I shove my feet into the wound
I go around wearing the wound
Or maybe the wound gets around, carrying smelly shoes
The wound is a pus mold made just for me

Shoes made of wound have flowers all over
When I shove my feet in the shoes, dark-pink globules
are crushed
Shoes made of wound are a chicken's throat, a chicken with
its belly cut open
When I shove my feet in, small rib bones break off
Shoes made of wound are an open grave
When I shove my feet in, my left foot my right foot
have on mommy's and daddy's graves

Wound's shoes get hysterical at times, but they are
patient overall
Blisters burst and rotten stench mushrooms
They bite down on my filthy feet, their pink lips tightly shut
My feet don't know whether the shoes are in pain or not

Wound's shoes have no sense of direction
Over there is always here and here is over there
Wound's shoes insist that every place I step is here
Whatever wound's shoes step on, that's my spot for
the moment
When the shoes become huge the feet become huge too
I wear shoes that have become as big as a hot rice sack
and jump like a white pig running away with its belly cut open

Shoes made of wound are full of rice
I shove my feet into the pot of perfectly cooked rice
Rice gets crushed like tiny roe under my feet
Shoes made of wound are mommy's sagging breasts
When the shoes touch the ground, they leave milky tear marks!
The sensation of shoving my stinky toes into someone's
warm throat that has
swarms of flies stuck to it

Right now, I'm walking in the scorching sun, wearing
wounds slanted outwards

(Translated by Don Mee Choi)

생일

아침에 눈 뜨면
침대에 가시가 가득해요
음악을 들을 땐
스피커에서 가시가 쏟아져요
나 걸어가면
발밑에 쌓이던 가시들
아무래도 내가 시계가 되었나봐요
내 몸에서 뾰족한 초침들이
솟아나나 봐요
그 초침들이
안타깝다
안타깝다
나를 찌르나 봐요
밤이 오면 자욱하게 비 내리는 초침 속을 헤치고
백 살 이백 살 걸어가 보기도 해요

저 먼 곳에
너무 멀어 환한 그 곳에
당신과 내가 살고 있다고
아주 행복하다고

당신 생일 날
그 초침들로 만든 케이크와 촛불로
안부 전해요

生日

早晨睁开眼睛
床上长满了刺
听音乐的时候
喇叭里冒出刺
当我走路
脚下堆满了刺
也许是我变成了钟表
我的身体里冒出
锋利的秒针
那些秒针 刺向我
你好可怜
你好可怜
夜晚我穿过细雨蒙蒙的秒针
走上一百年，二百年

遥远的地方
遥远到灿烂的地方
住着你和我
据说很幸福

你生日那天
我用秒针做成的蛋糕和蜡烛
为你祝福

Birthday

When I open my eyes in the morning
my bed is full of thorns
When I listen to music
thorns spill out from the speakers
When I walk
thorns pile up beneath my feet
I must have become a watch
Pointed second hands
protrude from my body
They needle me, saying
You poor thing
You poor thing
I walk through the second hands raining down at night
till I'm one hundred, two hundred years old

Over there faraway
so remote that the place shines out
that you and I live there
that we are very happy

I send you my regards
on your birthday
with cake and candles
made from those second hands

(Translated by Don Mee Choi)

내 안의 소금 원피스

슬픔을 참으면 몸에서 소금이 난다
짜디짠 당신의 표정
일평생 바다의 격렬한 타격에 강타당한 외로운 섬
같은 짐승의 눈빛

짧은 속눈썹 울타리 사이
파랑주의보 높아 바닷물 들이치는 날도 있었지만
소금의 건축이 허물어지지는 않았다
따가운 흐느낌처럼 손끝에서 피던 소금꽃

소금, 내 고꾸라진 그림자를 가루내어 가로등 아
　　래 뿌렸다
소금, 내 몸속에서 유전하는 바다의 건축

소금, 우리는 부둥켜안고 서로의
몸속에서 바다를 채집하려 했다

오늘은 일어나자마자 염전이 문을 열었다
나는 아침부터 바다의 건축이 올라오는 소리 듣는다

나는 몸속에 입었다
소금 원피스 한 벌

我身体里的盐裙

如果忍受悲伤，身体里会冒出盐
你的表情咸得令人不寒而栗
那是野兽的目光
犹如生生世世遭受大海打击的孤岛

短睫毛的篱笆之间
有时浪高，潮水汹涌
盐的建筑却没有倒塌
盐花在指尖绽放，像炽热的呜咽

盐。研磨我的倒影，撒在路灯之下
盐。在我的身体里游转的海的建筑

盐。我们紧紧拥抱，试图
从对方的身体里采集大海

今天刚起床，盐店开门了
我从早晨就听见大海建筑上升的声音

我在身体里穿上
一套盐裙

The Salt Dress Inside Me

When sorrow is endured, salt gets excreted from your body
Your salty-salty expression
Your animal gaze
like a lonely island hammered by the sea

Some days when there is a high-sea warning
seawater gushes in over the short eyelash fences
but the salt's architecture doesn't crumble
salt-flowers bloom from my fingertips like stinging sobs

Salt, turns my fallen shadow into powder and scatters it
under the streetlamps
Salt, persists in me like the sea's architecture

Salt, we embrace tightly and try
to capture the sea in each other

The salt pond is at work as soon as I'm awake
I listen to the rising sea architecture

I am wearing the salt dress
inside me

(Translated by Don Mee Choi)

탑승객

동그란 커피 동그란 수프 동그란 국수
동그란 윤회 동그란 것만 보면 속이 울렁거려

엄마의 안경알 속에서 아기가 부화한다
아기가 겨드랑이를 긁적이더니 사타구니를 긁적
인다

아기의 사타구니 속에서 엄마가 부화한다

거울 속에서 거울이 끝없이 거울이
햇살 속에서 햇살이 끝없이 햇살이

당신과 내가 부둥켜안은 알이 부화한다

약병에서 아스피린이 부화한다
천정에 붙은 물방울이 부화한다
구더기들이 부화한다
미끄덩거리는 올챙이가 부화한다

다음 생엔 브라만으로 태어나세요 다음 생엔 남자로 태어나세요
나를 속이려는 동그란 말 나를 속이려는 우주의 동그란 궤적들

내 방을 유영하는 잠의 비행선에서 내가 부화한다
잠옷을 입은 체 끌려나온 탑승자의 몸에서 비린내가 난다
아직 다 부화하지 못한 내 유령에서 아가미 냄새가 난다

잘 자라 우리 엄마 앞뜰과 뒷동산에 새들과 엄마 양과
엄마를 재워 다오 한번 엄마는 영원히 엄마 엄마를 재워다오

동그라미는 싫어 순환하는 건 싫어 낮 다음에 밤이 싫어
동그라미 같은 세상이라는 말은 누군가 나를 속이려는 말
알 낳고 그 알 품은 여자를 속이려는 말

밤에 갇힌 낮 낮에 갇힌 생선 생선에 갇힌 알 속
에 갇힌 불면증 내가 소리친다
잠의 비행선에 탑승하고 싶어 발버둥치는 사람이
소리친다

동그라미는 싫어 정말 싫어 이곳이 대합실이라고
말하는 자들이 싫어
동그란 국물 동그란 빗물 동그란 계란 정말 싫어
모두 사라지고 나면 다시 동그란 그릇 다시 동그
란 식탁

그릇 속의 물이 싫어
쇠나팔 속에서 올라오는 동그란 소리들 싫어

동그란 몸속에서 튀어나오려는 물감을 틀어쥐고
가쁜 숨 몰아쉬는 사람이 소리친다

정말 싫어!

乘客

圆圆的咖啡圆圆的勺子圆圆的面条
圆圆的轮回每次看见圆我都会恶心

妈妈的镜片里孵化出婴儿
婴儿挠着腋窝，挠着胯下

婴儿的胯下孵化出妈妈

在镜子里，镜子永远是镜子
在阳光下，阳光永远是阳光

你和我拥抱的蛋在孵化

药瓶里的阿司匹林在孵化
紧贴天花板的水滴在孵化
蛆虫在孵化
滑不溜秋的蝌蚪在孵化

下辈子做婆罗门吧下辈子做男人吧
圆圆的话语欺骗我，圆圆的宇宙轨迹欺骗我

睡眠的飞船漂浮在我的房间我在飞船里孵化
身穿睡衣被拉出来的乘客浑身腥臭
尚未完全孵化的我的幽灵散发着鱼鳃的气味

睡吧，我的妈妈，夜空里星光多灿烂
一日为母，终生为母。妈妈，睡吧

我讨厌圆讨厌循环讨厌白昼后的黑夜
世界像圆圈是别人用来欺骗我的说法
也用来欺骗产卵和孵卵的女人

关在黑夜里的白昼关在白昼里的鱼关在鱼里的卵关在卵
　　里的失眠症我呐喊
挣扎着要乘坐睡眠飞船的人在呐喊

我讨厌圆，真的讨厌。我讨厌说这里是候机大厅的人
圆圆的汤圆圆的雨圆圆的鸡蛋，真的讨厌
一切消失之后又是圆圆的碗，又是圆圆的餐桌

我讨厌碗里的水
讨厌铁喇叭里升起的圆圆的声音

揪住试图跳出圆圆身体的水彩，气喘吁吁的人在呼喊

真讨厌！

Passengers

Round coffee round soup round noodles
round samsara I feel nauseous whenever I see anything round

An infant hatches inside mommy's glasses
The infant scratches its armpits then scratches its crotch

Mommy hatches inside the infant's crotch

Inside the mirror the mirror endlessly the mirror
Inside the sunlight the sunlight endlessly the sunlight

The egg that you and I embrace hatches

Aspirin hatches inside the bottle
The drop of water stuck onto the ceiling hatches Maggots hatch
Slimy tadpoles hatch
Frogs spring up

In your next life please come back as a Brahman, in your
next life please come back as a man
The round words deceive me, the round wheel tracks of the
universe deceive me

I hatch inside sleep's airship that floats around in my room
The passenger who gets dragged out, still in pajamas, smells fishy
My specter that has not fully hatched smells like gills

Lullaby, and good night, in the skies stars are bright
Please put mommy to sleep once a mommy always a
mommy please put mommy to sleep

I hate the circle I hate circulating I hate the day then
the night
The world is like a circle—with these words someone is
trying to deceive me
and the women who lay eggs and brood them to keep them
laying eggs

The day trapped in the night the fish trapped in the day
the eggs trapped in the fish and the insomniac me
trapped inside the eggs is shouting
Someone who is desperate to get on the airship of sleep is yelling

I hate the circle really hate it I hate those who say this place
is a waiting room
Round soup round raindrop round egg I really hate them
After everything disappears there is the round bowl again
the round table again

I hate the water in the bowl
I hate the round sounds emitted from the trumpet

Someone pants and grips the dye about to pop out of the
round body and shouts

I really hate it!

(Translated by Don Mee Choi)

양파

남자가 수도꼭지 아래서 여자의 껍질을 벗겼어
여자는 깔깔거리며 양파처럼 잘도 벗겨졌어
어두운 밤이 한꺼풀 벗겨지자 투명한 낮이 솟아올랐어
신선한 알의 물컹한 속처럼
배수관을 타고 피가 쭉쭉 빨려나갔어
그러지마그러지마 느네들 왜 그래 누군가 울었어
낮을 쪽쪽 빨아먹으면 슬픈맛매운맛 밤이 솟아오르고
천년만년 세세무궁 낮밤은 그 짓을 되풀이했건만
여자는 훌러덩 훌러덩 잘도 벗겨졌어
양파를 벗기던 남자는 눈이 매워서 울었어 여자도 덩달아 울었어
아 그리고그래서그럼에도 오늘 낮이 가고 밤이 왔건만
나는 어디 있었는지 매운 껍질의 갈피 어디숨겨져 있었는지
자꾸만 물어보다 돌아보면 여자의 몸은 다시그대로
남자는 울면서 자꾸만 울면서 여자의 껍질을 벗겼어

양파처럼 다 벗겨지고나니 나는 없는데
나를 나라고 부르던 나는 어디 숨어 있었던것
　　인지
매운 껍질들 다 벗어놓고 밤은 마룻장 밑에숨어서
　　떨기만 하는데
저 바다는 바지를 벗었다가 또 입었다가 한없이
　　그러는데
여름엔더웠고 겨울엔추웠어 모두모두 흘러가 버
　　렸어
세상에서제일아름다운이야기지?

洋葱

男人在水龙头下剥去女人的外壳
女人咯咯笑着像洋葱被轻易剥光
漆黑的夜被剥开，冒出透明的白昼
像新鲜鸡蛋稀烂的内部
沿着排水管鲜血被汩汩吸走
别这样别这样你们怎么了，有人哭泣
吸食白昼会冒出夜晚，或悲伤或辛辣
千年万年，世世代代，昼夜反复
女人总是那么容易被剥光
剥洋葱的男人被辣哭了，女人也跟着哭
啊，而且，所以，尽管，这个白昼过去，黑夜来临
我在哪儿，我藏在辛辣外壳的哪个位置
不停地问，转头看时，女人的身体又恢复原样
男人在哭，不停地哭着剥掉女人的外壳

像洋葱一样剥完之后，我不见了
称我为我的我藏到哪里了
辛辣的外壳统统剥光，黑夜藏在地板之下
不停地颤抖
大海脱下裤子又穿上，一次又一次
夏天热冬天冷，一切都流走了
这是不是世界上最美丽的故事？

Onion

Under the faucet a man peeled a woman's skin
The woman cacklecackled and peeled easily like an onion
As a layer of dark night peeled off transparent day soared
Blood draindrained down a pipe
        like the mushy inside of a fresh egg
Someone cried, stop it stop it why are you all acting this way?
When day gets suckled the sad tasting spicy tasting night soars
Day and night kept this up for a thousand ten thousand
        years, for all eternity
yet the woman peeled layer after layer
The man who peeled an onion cried because of its sap
        and the woman cried along with him
ah and so regardless today's day left and night arrived
        yet I didn't know where I was
maybe I was hidden somewhere between the spicy layers
so when I kept asking where I was and turned around
        the woman's body was just as before
and the man kept crying and crying and peeled the woman's skin

After I was all peeled like an onion, I wasn't there anymore
but the I that used to call me I was hiding somewhere
Night hid and trembled under the wood floor after taking
        off its spicy skin
yet the sea endlessly took off and put on a pair of pants
and yet it was hot in summer and cold in winter and
        everything drifted away
Isn't this the most beautiful story in the world?

(Translated by Don Mee Choi)

作者简介

金惠顺，生于韩国，在建国大学取得韩国文学博士学位。1979 年开始发表诗歌，在《文学与文智》杂志上发表了《诗人抽烟》等五首诗。此后出版了十本诗集，包括《来自别的恒星》（1981）、《父亲的稻草人》（1984）、《某恒星的地狱》（1987）、《我们的负片照》（1991）、《首尔，我的奥义书》（1994）、《可怜的爱情机器》（1997）、《给日历工厂经理》（2000）、《一杯红玻璃》（2004）、《你的第一次》（2008）、《忧郁牙膏和玻璃镜奶油》（2011）等。她的诗被翻译成英文出版的有《妈妈肯定是一个羽毛喷泉》（2008）和《全世界的垃圾，集结起来！》（2011）。她获得的奖项包括“金洙暎文学奖”（1997）、“素月诗文学奖”（2000）、“未堂文学奖”（2006） 等。现居首尔，于首尔艺术大学教授创意写作。

Kim Hyesoon was born in South Korea. She received her Ph.D. in Korean Literature from Konkuk University. Beginning as a poet in 1979 with the publication of "Poet Smoking a Cigarette" and four other poems in Literature and Intellect, she has published ten poetry collections including: *From Another Star* (1981), *My Father's Scarecrow* (1984), *The Hell of a Certain Star* (1987), *The Negative of Our Picture* (1991), *My Upanishad, Seoul* (1994), *Poor Love Machine* (1997), *To the Calendar Factory Manager* (2000), *A Glass of Red Mirror* (2004), *Your First* (2008), and *Sorrowtoothpaste Mirrorcream* (2011). Her poetry collections have been translated into English, including *Mommy Must be a Fountain of Feathers* (2008), and *All the Garbage of the World, Unite!* (2011). She has received numerous literary prizes including the Kim Su-Yong Literary Award (1997), the Sowol Poetry Literature Award (2000) and the Midang Literature Award (2006). She lives in Seoul and teaches creative writing at the Seoul Institute of Arts.

图书在版编目（CIP）数据

我身体里的盐裙：朝、汉、英 / (韩) 金惠顺著；薛舟译. -- 南京：江苏凤凰文艺出版社, 2021.1

(红狐丛书. 一衣带水的相望)

ISBN 978-7-5594-1387-1

Ⅰ. ①我… Ⅱ. ①金… ②薛… Ⅲ. ①诗集－韩国－现代－朝鲜语、汉语、英语 Ⅳ. ①I312.625

中国版本图书馆CIP数据核字(2019)第160949号

红狐丛书·一衣带水的相望：我身体里的盐裙

北岛 主编
(韩) 金惠顺 著
薛舟 译

出 版 人　张在健
责任编辑　王娱瑶　于奎潮
特约编辑　薛　倩　傅春晖
书籍设计　周伟伟
责任印制　刘　巍
出版发行　江苏凤凰文艺出版社
　　　　　南京市中央路165号，邮编：210009
出版社网址　http://www.jswenyi.com
印　　刷　苏州越洋印刷有限公司
开　　本　880×1230毫米　1/32
印　　张　3.75
字　　数　40千字
版　　次　2021年1月第1版
印　　次　2021年1月第1次印刷
标准书号　ISBN 978-7-5594-1387-1
定　　价　128.00元（全七册）

红狐丛书·东亚卷 | 北岛 主编

新奇啊，新奇，每个阳光灿烂的夜晚

Amazing, How Amazing It Is,
Every Night of the Shining Sun

신기하다, 신기해,
햇빛 찬연한 밤마다

Lee Seong-bok

［韩］李晟馥 著 薛舟 谢小婷 译

江苏凤凰文艺出版社
JIANGSU PHOENIX LITERATURE AND ART PUBLISHING

目录

Contents

Amazing, How Amazing It Is, Every Night of the Shining Sun

Lee Seong-bok

1959년

그해 겨울이 지나고 여름이 시작되어도
봄은 오지 않았다 복숭아나무는
채 꽃 피기 전에 아주 작은 열매를 맺고
不姙의 살구나무는 시들어 갔다
소년들의 性器에는 까닭없이 고름이 흐르고
의사들은 아프리카까지 移民을 떠났다 우리는
유학 가는 친구들에게 술 한잔 얻어 먹거나
이차 대전 때 南洋으로 징용 간 삼촌에게서
뜻밖의 편지를 받기도 했다 그러나 어떤
놀라움도 우리를 無氣力과 不感症으로부터
불러내지 못했고 다만, 그 전해에 비해
약간 더 화려하게 절망적인 우리의 습관을
修飾했을 뿐 아무 것도 追憶되지 않았다
어머니는 살아 있고 여동생은 발랄하지만
그들의 기쁨은 소리 없이 내 구둣발에 짓이겨
지거나 이미 파리채 밑에 으깨어져 있었고
春畫를 볼 때마다 부패한 채 떠올라 왔다

그해 겨울이 지나고 여름이 시작되어도
우리는 봄이 아닌 倫理와 사이비 學說과
싸우고 있었다 오지 않는 봄이어야 했기에
우리는 보이지 않는 監獄으로 자진해 갔다

1959年

那年冬天过后就是夏天
春天没有来　桃树
还没开花就结出小小的果实
不孕的杏树枯萎了
少年们的性器无缘无故地流出脓水
医生们移民非洲　出国
留学的朋友请我们喝酒
意外地收到二战期间
被征到南洋的叔叔的信　任何
惊讶都不能将我们从无力和麻木中
唤醒　我们只是
修饰着比前年更华丽的绝望习惯
没有任何回忆
妈妈还活着　妹妹活力四射
她们的喜悦却被我的皮鞋无声地践踏
或者早已捻碎在苍蝇拍下
每次看春画的时候才会腐朽地涌起

那年冬天过后就是夏天
我们和没有春天的逻辑斗争　和似是而非
的学说斗争　春天还是没有来
我们自觉地走向看不见的监狱

1959

That year, though winter ended and summer began
spring did not come   The peach tree
bore tiny fruits before flowering
and the barren apricot withered
For unknown reasons pus oozed from the penises of young boys
and doctors emigrated as far as Africa   We were treated to drinks by
friends leaving to study abroad
and out of the blue a letter arrived from an uncle drafted
and sent to the South Pacific during World War Two   but there were
no surprises to roust us from our indifference and apathy
and other than glamorizing,
even more than last year, our habitual depression,
we did nothing worth remembering
Mom was still alive and my younger sister full of life,
yet without a peep from them their happiness was squashed,
beneath my shoes, by flyswatters—a memory that surfaced,
rotten, whenever I saw a salacious picture

Though winter ended and summer began
it wasn't the spring we wrestled with, but ethics
and false theories   It was a spring that did not come,
and so we voluntarily went off to an invisible jail

(Translated by Hye-jin Juhn Sidney & George Sidney)

出埃及

1

오늘 다 외로와하면
내일 씹을 괴로움이 안 남고
내일 마실 그리움이 안 남는다
오늘은 집에 돌아가자 세편의 映畫를 보고
두 명의 주인공이 살해되는 꼴을 보았으니
운좋게 살아남은 그 녀석을 너라 생각하고
집에 돌아가자, 살아 있으니
수줍어 말고 되돌아 취하지 말고 돌아가자
돌아가 싱싱한 떡잎으로 자라나서
훨훨 날아올라 충격도, 마약도 없이
꿈 속에서 한 편 映畫가 되어 펼쳐지자

2

내가 떠나기 전에 길은 제 길을 밟고
사라져 버리고, 길은 마른 오징어처럼
펴져 있고 돌이켜 술을 마시면
먼저 취해 길바닥에 드러눕는 愛人

나는 휑한 地下道에서 뜬눈을 새우다가
헛소리하며 찾아오는 東方博士들을
죽일까봐 겁이 난다

이제 집이 없는 사람은 天國에 셋방을 얻어야
하고
사랑받지 못하는 사람은 아직 欲情에 떠는 늙
은 子宮으로 돌아가야 하고
忿怒에 떠는 손에 닿으면 문둥이와 앉은뱅이까
지 낫는단다, 主여

出埃及

一

今天的孤独享尽之后
就不会留下明天咀嚼的痛苦
也不会留下明天饮尝的思念
今天回家吧　看了三部电影
看到两名主人公被害的惨状
把那个幸存的家伙想成是你
回家吧、既然你还活着
就不要害羞　不要喝醉　回家吧
回家　长成茂盛的子叶
翩翩飞舞　没有冲击　没有毒品
成为一部电影　展现在梦里

二

我出发之前　路踩着自己的路
消失　路像干鱿鱼
延伸　转弯　每次喝酒
总是醉卧在路边的爱人

我在空荡荡的地下道里彻夜未眠
我害怕
自己会杀死胡言乱语找来的东方博士

如今没有家的人只能在天国租房
得不到爱的人只能回到仍在情欲中颤抖的衰老的子宫
只要碰到因愤怒而颤抖的手　麻风病人和瘫子也能痊愈，
主啊

Exodus

1

If you consume all your loneliness today
you won't have any pain left to chew on tomorrow
you won't have any longing left to drink tomorrow
As for today, let's go home   You've watched three films
and seen two main characters murdered
So let me think the lucky one who survived is you
and let's go home   You're alive, so
let's not be self-conscious or go off to get drunk but let's go
home and then fresh as young leaves   Let's
fly up to the sky   not from drugs, or from the shocks
we've had, but
from our dreams let's spin out a movie

2

Even before I start off the road, treading on itself,
vanishes   It lies flat like dried squid
I turn back and drink
My girl friend gets drunk first and sprawls on the ground

I'm afraid that having stayed awake all night
in the murk of an underpass I'll kill the Three Wise Men
when they come talking nonsense

Now those who don't have homes should rent rooms in
heaven
and those who aren't loved should return to old wombs still
quivering with lust
and even lepers and cripples will be cured if touched by a
hand that shakes with wrath, my Lord

(Translated by Hye-jin Juhn Sidney & George Sidney)

여름산

여름산은 솟아 오른다
熱氣와 金屬의 투명한 옷자락을 끌어 올리며
솟아 오른다 발등에 못 안 박힌 것들은 다 솟
　　아 오른다 저기
비행기가 수술톱처럼 하늘을 끊어낸다 은빛 날
　　개가 곤두선다
그 여자는 佛蘭西에 가겠다고 이번 여름엔 꼭
다녀와야겠다고 그 여자는 잠자는 벌레를 밟았
　　다 모르고
밟았다 부서지면서 물 같은 피가 솟아 올랐
　　다 내가 거듭 밟았다
그 여자는 佛蘭西에 가겠다고

나는 속으로 욕했다
따지고 보면 욕할 이유가 없었다
당신은 남의 가난이 얼마큼 당신과 관계 있다
　　고 생각합니까
그 여자는 내가 가난한 사람이 아니라고 말했다
당신은 백 사람 중에 하나가 병들어 아프면 당
　　신도 아프다고 생각합니까
그 여자는 부질없는 말이라고 대답했다

여름산은 솟아 오른다
여름산은 땀 흘리지 않는다 힘쓰지 않는다
여름산 여름산 여름산 우리는 그늘에서 콜라를 마셨다
콜라를 마시며 佛蘭西를 생각하고 울었다 우는 시늉을 했다
우리는, 시멘트 포를 등에 지고 사다리 오르는 여인들을 생각하며 울었다
우는 흉내를 냈다 우리는, 바빌론에 묶여 있는 이스라엘 사람들을 생각하며 울었다 우는 척했다

여름산은 솟아 오른다
한숨 쉬지 않고 솟아 오른다 반짝임과 몽롱함을 뿌리며 솟아 오른다
우리는 손을 잡았다 잡힌 손에서 물 같은 피가 흘렀다 살려줘요!

여름산은 무겁게 솟아 오른다
솟아 오르지 않는다 솟아 오르는 모습만 보여 준다
여름산 여름산 여름산 먼지, 매연, 악취로 부서지는

여름산 여름산
여름산

夏天的山

夏天的山高耸
掀起热气和金属的透明衣角
高耸　脚背没钉钉子的东西全部高耸
飞机像手术刀　切开天空　竖起银翼

她说要去法兰西　今年夏天
非去不可　她踩到睡着的虫子却不知道
虫子被踩碎　冒出水似的血　我又踩上了
她说要去法兰西

我在心里咒骂
仔细想来　我没理由骂人
你认为别人的贫穷和你有什么关系
她说我不是穷人
百分之一的人生病　你会感觉痛苦吗
她说这是无稽之谈

夏天的山高耸
夏天的山努力不流汗
夏天的山　夏天的山　夏天的山　我们在阴凉里喝可乐

喝着可乐　想着法兰西哭泣　模仿哭泣
我们，想到背着水泥袋爬梯子的女人而哭泣
模仿哭泣　我们想到被绑在巴比伦的以色列人而哭泣
假装哭泣

夏天的山高耸
一刻不停地高耸　喷洒着璀璨和朦胧　高耸
我们手拉手　手里流出水样的鲜血　救命啊！

夏天的山沉重地高耸
不是高耸　只是显出高耸的模样
夏天的山　夏天的山　夏天的山　因为灰尘　煤烟和恶臭

而粉碎的夏天的山　夏天的山
夏天的山

The Summer Mountain

The summer mountain rises
dragging along its transparent vestments of heat and metal
it rises   all whose feet are not nailed down rise too
above, like a surgical saw a plane rips the sky   its silver
wings angled upward

The woman insisted she'd go to France   she'd go this
summer
for sure   she stepped on a sleeping bug   not knowing
it was there
She stepped on it   as it cracked, liquid like blood shot
up   I too
stepped on it   she insisted she would go to France

I felt critical of her
but reflecting on it there was no reason to be critical of her
How much does the poverty of others mean to you?
She said I wasn't poor

If only one in a hundred is sick and in pain, can you also feel the pain?
Senseless questions, she said

The summer mountain rises
The summer mountain doesn't sweat   it doesn't exert itself
The summer mountain   the summer mountain   the summer mountain   we drank cola in the shade
As we drank we cried, thinking of France   we pretended to cry
We cried thinking of the working women climbing ladders with sacks of cement on their backs
We pretended to cry   We cried thinking of the
        Israelites in captivity in Babylon   We pretended to cry

The summer mountain rises
without taking a breath it rises   shattering shadow and light it rises
We held each other's hands   blood flowed from our hands   help!

The summer mountain rises ponderously
It doesn't rise   it generates the illusion that it is rising
The summer mountain   the summer mountain   the summer
        mountain obliterated by dust, exhaust fumes, toxic stench
the summer mountain   the summer mountain
the summer mountain

(Translated by Hye-jin Juhn Sidney & George Sidney)

그해 가을

그해 가을 나는 아무에게도 便紙 보내지 않았
　　지만
늙어 軍人 간 친구의 便紙 몇 통을 받았다 세
　　상 나무들은
어김없이 동시에 물들었고 풀빛을 지우며 집들
　　은 언덕을
뻗어나가 하늘에 이르렀다 그해 가을 濟州産 5
　　년생 말은
제 주인에게 대드는 자가용 운전사를 물어뜯었
　　고 어느
유명 작가는 南美紀行文을 연재했다
아버지, 아버지가 여기 계실 줄 몰랐어요
그해 가을 소꿉장난은 國産映畫 보다 시들했으
　　며 길게
하품하는 입은 더 깊고 울창했다 깃발을 올리거
　　나 내릴
때마다 말뚝처럼 사람들은 든든하게 박혔지
　　만 햄머
휘두르는 소리, 들리지 않았다 그해 가을 모래
　　내 앞
샛강에 젊은 뱀장어가 떠오를 때 파헤쳐진 샛강
　　도 둥둥

떠올랐고 高架道路 공사장의 한 사내는 새 깃
털과 같은
速度로 떨어져내렸다 그해 가을 개들이 털갈이
할 때
지난 여름 번데기 사 먹고 죽은 아이들의 어머
니는 후미진
골목길을 서성이고 실성한 늙은이와 天賦의 白
痴는
서울역이나 창경원에 버려졌다 그해 가을 한 승
려는
人骨로 만든 피리를 불며 密教僧이 되어 돌아
왔고 내가
만날 시간을 정하려 할 때 그 여자는 침을 뱉
고 돌아섰다
아버지, 새벽에 나가 꿈 속에 돌아오던 아버지,
여기 묻혀 있을 줄이야
그해 가을 나는 세상에서 재미 못 봤다는 투
의 말버릇은
버리기로 결심했지만 이 결심도 농담 이상의 것
은
아니었다 떨어진 은행잎이나 나둥그러진 매미
를 주워

성냥갑 속에 모아두고 나도 누이도 房門을 안
으로잠갔다 그해 가을 나는 어떤 가을
도 그해의 것이
아님을 알았으며 아무것도 美化시키지 않기 위
해서는
卑下시키지도 않는 法을 배워야 했다
아버지, 아버지! 내가 네 아버지냐
그해 가을 나는 살아온 날들과 살아갈 날들
을 다 살아
버렸지만 壁에 맺힌 물방울 같은 또 한 女子
를 만났다
그 여자가 흩어지기 전까지 세상 모든 눈들
이 감기지
않을 것을 나는 알았고 그래서 그레고르 잠자
의 家族들이
移葬을 끝내고 소풍 갈 준비를 하는 것을 이해
했다
아버지, 아버지…… 씹새끼, 너는 입이 열이라
도 말 못해
그해 가을, 假面 뒤의 얼굴은 假面이었다

那年秋天

那年秋天　我没有给谁写过信
却收到几封来自老了才去参军的朋友的信　世上的树木
不约而同地同时染色　抹掉了绿　房子沿着山坡
伸展　直达天空　那年秋天　产自济州的五年生马匹
咬了顶撞主人的车夫　某个
著名作家在连载《南美纪行文》
父亲，我不知道父亲在这里
那年秋天　过家家比国产电影还无聊　长长地
打着哈欠的嘴更加深邃和苍茫　每当升旗降旗
的时候　人们就像牢牢钉紧的木桩　却听不见
挥舞锤子的声音　那年秋天　当小鳗鱼浮上
沙河前的沙洲　被挖开的沙洲

也悠悠浮起　在高架路施工现场　一个男人
以羽毛的速度坠落　那年秋天　狗换毛的时候
夏天吃蛹而死的孩子们的妈妈在僻静的
胡同里徘徊　精神失常的老人和天生的白痴
被人抛弃在首尔火车站和昌庆苑　那年秋天　一位和尚
吹着用人骨做成的笛子　变成密教僧侣归来
我要确定见面的时间　那个女人啐了口唾沫　转过身去
父亲，清晨出门又在梦中归来的父亲，
谁能想到他会被埋在这里
那年秋天　我决心要改掉这个世界真没劲
的口头禅　不过这决心也只是
开个玩笑　我捡起凋零的银杏叶和跌落的蝉

积攒在火柴盒里　我和姐姐反锁了房门
那年秋天　我知道哪个秋天也不属于
那一年　为了不美化任何事物
我必须学会不丑化的方法
父亲，父亲！我是你的父亲吗
那年秋天　从前的日子和未来的日子
我都已过完　却遇到了像是墙上凝结的水珠的女人
我知道　那个女人消散之前　世界上所有的眼睛
都不会关闭　我理解格雷戈尔·萨姆沙的家人们　移葬结束
做好了出门郊游的准备
父亲，父亲……兔崽子，你跳进黄河也洗不清了
那年秋天　面具背后的脸还是面具

That Fall

That fall though I didn't send anybody a letter   I got
several from
friends who'd gone off to do the obligatory military service
they'd been
postponing   All the trees in the world turned yellow at
the same time,
as usual, and houses scaled the hillside right up to the sky,
overwhelming
the color of grass   that fall a five-year-old Cheju Island
pony bit
Somebody's private chauffeur arguing with its owner, and a
well-known
writer serialized some travel pieces about his journey to
South America
Dad, I didn't realize you were going to be here
That fall the children playing house were more tedious even
than
Korean films, and the long drawn-out yawns were
heavier   whenever we
raised the flag or lowered it people were driven like posts
into the ground,
but the sound of a hammer wasn't heard   that fall when
a dead

young eel floated to the surface of the stream in front of
Moraenae,
the stream, which had been dredged, also floated, and a
worker fell
at the speed of a feather from the elevated expressway that
was being
built   That fall when dogs changed coats, the mother of
the children
who'd died the previous summer after eating sautéed
silkworm larvae
bought from a sidewalk vendor, hung out on dark
        street corners
A senile old man was abandoned at the Seoul
        train station,
as was a congenital idiot at the Changgyeong
Palace   That fall a
Buddhist monk returned as a mystic, playing a flute made of
human
bone, and when I asked a woman for a date she spit and
turned away
My father, who used to leave home in the early morning and
come back
in my dreams, how would I have known he was
        buried here

That fall I decided to break my habit of talking as though
there wasn't
any fun in my life, but even that decision turned out to be
no more
than a joke   I picked up fallen ginkgo leaves and dead
cicadas and kept
them in match boxes, and my sister and I locked our rooms
from inside
That fall I realized there was no fall that belonged to any
particular year
and I taught myself not to debase things so as not to
beautify them
Dad, Dad! Am I your dad
That fall I lived all the days I'd lived, and those I was going
to live
but I met another woman, who was like a drop of
        water clinging
to a wall, and I realized that not an eye in all the world
would close
until she splattered, so I understood why Gregor
        Samsa's family
prepared to go on an outing after burying him
Dad, Dad ... you little fucker, you should be too ashamed to
talk
That fall, the face behind the mask was a mask

(Translated by Hye-jin Juhn Sidney & George Sidney)

세월에 대하여

1

石手의 삶은 돌을 깨뜨리고 채소 장수의 삶은
하루 종일 서 있다 몬티를 닮은 내 친구는
同時上映館에서 죽치더니 또 어디로 갔는지
세월은 갔고 세월은 갈 것이고 이천 년 되는 해
아침 나는 孫子를 볼 것이다 그래 가야지
天國으로 통하는 車들은 바삐 지나가고
가로수는 줄을 잘 맞춘다 저기, 웬 아이가
쥐꼬리를 잡고 빙빙 돌리며 씽긋 웃는다
세월이여, 얼어붙은 날들이여
야근하고 돌아와 환한 날들을 잠자던 누이들이여

2

피로의 물줄기를 타넘다 보면 때로 이마에
뱀딸기꽃이 피어 오르고 그건 대부분
幻影이었고 때로는 정말 형님이 아들을 낳기도
했다 아버지가 으흐허 웃었다 발가벗은
나무에서 또 몇 개의 열매가 떨어졌다 때로는
얼음 깔린 하늘 위로 붉은 말이 연탄을
끌고 갔다 그건 대부분 幻影이었고 정말
허리 꺾인 아이들이 철 지난 고추나무처럼

언덕에 박혀 있기도 했다 정말 去勢된
친구들이 유행가를 부르며 사라져 갔지만
세월은 흩날리지 않았다 세월은 신다 버린 구두
속에서 곤한 잠을 자다 들키기도 하고
때로는 총알 맞은 새처럼 거꾸로 떨어졌다
아버지는 으흐허 웃고만 있었다 피로의 물줄기를
타넘다 보면 때로 나는 높은 새집 위에서
잠시 쉬기도 하였고 그건 대부분 幻影이었다

3

세월은 갔고 아무도 그 어둡고 깊은 노린내 나는
구멍으로부터 돌아오지 못했다 몇 번인가 되돌아온
便紙 해답은 언제나 질문의 殘骸였고 친구들은
태엽 풀린 비행기처럼 고꾸라지곤 했다 너무
피곤해 手淫을 할 수 없을 때 어른거리던
하얀 풀뿌리 얼어붙은 웅덩이 세월은 갔고
매일매일 작부들은 노래 불렀다 스물 세 살,
스물 네 살 나이가 담뱃진에 노랗게 물들 때까지
또 나는 열 한 시만 되면 버스를 집어 탔고
세월은 갔다 봉제 공장 누이들이 밥 먹는 30 분 동안
다리미는 세워졌고 어느 예식장에서나 30 분마다

신랑 신부는 바뀌어 갔다 세월은 갔다 변색한
백일 사진 華僑들의 공동묘지 싸구려 밥집 빗물
고인 길바닥, 나뭇잎에도 세월은 갔다 한 아이가
세발 자전거를 타고 번잡한 찻길을 가고 있었다
어떤 사람은 불쌍했고 어떤 사람은 불쌍한
사람을 보고 울었다 아무 것도 그 비리고 어지러운
숨막힌 구멍으로부터 돌아오지 못했다

4

나는 세월이란 말만 들으면 가슴이 아프다
나는 곱게곱게 자라왔고 몇 개의 돌부리 같은
事件들을 제외하면 아무 일도 없었다 중학교
고등학교 그 어려운 修業時代, 욕정과 영웅심과
부끄러움도 쉽게 風化했다 잊어버릴 것도 없는데
세월은 안개처럼, 醉氣처럼 올라온다
웬 들 판 이 이 렇 게 넓 어 지 고
얼마나빨간작은꽃들이지평선끝까지아물거리는가

그해
자주 눈이 내리고
빨리 흙탕물로 변해갔다
나는 밤이었다 나는 너와 함께

기차를 타고 민둥산을 지나가고 있
었다 이따금 기차가 멎으면 하얀 物體가
어른거렸고 또 기차는 떠났다 ...... 세월은 갔다

어쩌면 이런 일이 있었는지도 모른다

내가
돌아서
출렁거리는
어둠 속으로 빨려들어갈 때
너는 발을 동동 구르며
부서지기 시작했다
아무 소리도 들리지 않았다

(나는 너를 사랑했다
나는 네가 잠자는 두 평 房이었다
人形 몇 개가 같은 표정으로 앉아 있고
액자 속의 教會에서는 종소리가 들리
는 ...... 나는 너의 房이었다
네가 바라보는 풀밭이었다
풀밭 옆으로 숨죽여 흐르는 냇물이었다

그리고 나는 아무 것도 아니었다
문득 고개를 떨군 네
마음 같은,
한줌
空氣였다)

세월이라는 말이 어딘가에서 나를 발견할 때마다
하늘이 눈더미처럼 내려앉고 전깃줄 같은 것이
부들부들 떨고 있는 것을 본다 남들처럼
나도 두어 번 戀愛에 실패했고 그저 실패했을
뿐, 그때마다 유행가가 얼마만큼 절실한지
알았고 노는 사람이나 놀리는 사람이나 그리
행복하지 않다는 것을 알아야 했다 세월은
언제나 남보다 앞서 갔고 나는 또 몇 번씩
그 비좁고 습기찬 門間을 지나가야 했다

关于岁月

1

石匠的人生就是打碎石头　菜贩子的人生
是站立终日　酷似蒙蒂的朋友
泡在同时上映馆　这会儿不知去了哪里
岁月流逝　岁月还会继续流逝　已是两千年
的早晨　我会看到孙子　是的　我要去
通往天国的车忙忙碌碌
行道树排列整齐　那里　有个孩子
抓着老鼠尾巴团团转圈　面带微笑

岁月啊　冰封的日子
夜班归来　姐姐们在灿烂的白天酣然入睡

2

跨过疲惫的水柱　有时额头上
会开出蛇梅花　大部分
是幻影　有时哥哥真的会生孩子
父亲哈哈笑　赤裸裸的
树上又掉落几颗果实　有时
红马拉着煤炭走向冰封的天空
这些大部分是幻影
弯腰的孩子们真的像过季的辣椒秧

插满山坡　被阉割的朋友们真的
唱着流行歌曲消失　不过
岁月不会飘散　岁月在穿破扔掉的皮鞋里
熟睡　有时被发现
有时像中弹的小鸟　倒头跌落
父亲只是哈哈笑　跨过疲惫的水柱
有时我在高高的鸟巢里
休息片刻　这些大部分是幻影

3

岁月流逝　谁也不能从黑暗深邃而腥臭
的洞中返回　几次被退回的信
总是疑问的残骸　朋友们
就像发条松弛的飞机　倒栽下来
疲惫得无力手淫的时候　冰冻的水坑里
白色的草根在摇曳　岁月流逝
妓女们每天唱歌　直到二十三岁
二十四岁的年纪被香烟熏黄
每天夜里十一点　我就乘上公车
岁月流逝　缝纫机厂的姐姐们吃饭的三十分钟里
熨斗被竖起　无论是哪个礼堂　每隔三十分钟

新郎新娘都会被换掉　岁月流逝　褪色的
百日照　华侨公墓　廉价饭馆
积了雨水的路面　岁月也在树叶上流逝　一个孩子
骑着三轮自行车　经过杂乱的车道
有人很可怜　有人为可怜的人
哭泣　一切都不能从那血腥凌乱
令人窒息的洞中返回

4
我听到岁月这个字眼就会心痛
我从小备受宠爱　除了几块
绊脚石　基本上平安无事　中学
困难的学习时代　情欲和英雄心
以及羞耻都轻易地风化　没什么需要遗忘
岁月像雾，像醉意缭绕
为什么田野变得如此辽阔
那么红的小花轻轻摇曳直到地平线尽头

那年经常下雪
迅速地化作泥汤
我是黑夜　和你一起
乘坐火车　翻过荒山野岭

偶尔火车停下　白色的物体
闪烁　火车又开了……岁月流逝

也许发生过这样的事情

我
转身
被吸入
激荡的黑暗
你咚咚跺脚
开始粉碎
什么声音也听不见

（我爱你
我是你睡觉的两坪的房子
几个玩偶面带同样的表情端坐
镜框里的教堂　钟声响起……
我是你的房子
是你凝望的草地
是草地边屏息流淌的溪水

然而我什么都不是
我是
一缕空气
像你的心
当你忽然低头的时候）

当岁月这个词在某个地方发现我
天空如雪堆降落　电线似的东西
看着什么在瑟瑟发抖　像别人
我也两三次恋爱失败　失败而已
这时　我会知道流行歌曲是多么真实
我必须懂得　玩弄的人和被玩弄的人
都不幸福　岁月
总是走在别人前面　我还要几次
通过那个狭窄而潮湿的门槛

About Time

1

A mason's life is breaking stone and a grocer's life is standing
all day   My friend who looked like Montgomery Clift
used to
hang around a third-class double-feature movie house
I don't know what's become of him   Time has passed
and will
continue to pass   On the morning of the first day of the
year
two thousand I'll have a grandson   Well, I've got to
go   the cars
to paradise flash past, the roadside trees stand in
        straight rows
Over there a child grins, twirling a mouse by its tail

time, frozen days   Sisters who after working all night at
the factory
slept through sun-bright days

2

As I followed the river of weariness, from time to time
        on my

forehead a wild strawberry bloomed   most of that was
fantasy
In reality from time to time my elder brother sired a son
laughter burbled from my father   again some fruit fell
from a naked tree   from time to time a red
        horse crossed
the iced-over sky pulling a cartload of yeontan briquettes
most of that was fantasy   In reality some children, bent
double,
were rooted on a hill like red-pepper plants left uncollected
during
harvest   In reality my emasculated friends
        disappeared singing
current pop songs   but time did not fly away
It was sometimes found deeply asleep inside a worn
abandoned shoe
and from time to time it plummeted upside down
like a shot-gunned bird   laughter burbled from my father
as I followed the river of weariness from time to time I
rested
upon a bird's nest high up   most of that was fantasy too

3

Time passed and nobody was able to come back from the
deep dark
stinking hole   A letter was returned several times
answers were always
to be found in the debris of questions and friends would
give out
like toy airplanes with spent rubber-bands   when I was
too tired to
masturbate the white roots of grass in a frozen swamp swam
before
my eyes   time passed   the prostitutes sang songs
every day, and by the
time they were twenty-three, twenty-four, cigarettes had
stained them
yellow   and every night by eleven I caught the bus
    for home

And time passed   during the half hour the girls at
    the sewing
factory ate lunch the clothes irons stood cooling and every
half hour

in every wedding hall there was another bride and groom
time passed   in an infant's faded hundredth-day
photo   in a public
graveyard for Chinese immigrants   in a cheap
restaurant   on a road
where rainwater puddle   on leaves   time passed
on a street busy with traffic a child pedaled along on
        a tricycle
some people were miserable, some who saw them wept
Nothing could come back from the asphyxiating malodorous
dizzying hole

4

My heart aches whenever I hear the word time
I was brought up as a treasured child, and nothing
significant
happened to me other than my encountering in my path
a few stones that I got easily past—middle school,
        high school,
the difficult period of learning, and then lust, and a desire to
be heroic,
and feelings of shame   though there's nothing I need to

forget,
time rises like a fog, like drunkenness
how is it that the field grows so wide
and how is it that there are so many red flowers wavering
on the horizon

That year
snow fell often and
the road turned quickly muddy
I was night, I was on a train with you
passing a bare mountain   the train
from time to time stopped, something white
flickered, and the train moved on again … time passed

This also might have happened

when I
turned round
and sank into
the rolling darkness
stamping the ground
you began to break apart

not a sound

was heard

(I loved you

I was the two-pyeong room you were sleeping in

several dolls with the same face sat next to each other

and a bell tolled in the church inside a framed picture ...

I was your room

I was the grassy field you gazed at

I was the stream that ran quietly alongside the grassy field

and I was nothing

I was

a handful of air,

like your heart

when of a sudden you bow your head)

Whenever the word time comes upon me somewhere
I see the sky falling like an avalanche of snow
and something like an electric wire
vibrating   like others
I several times failed at love   each time was only
a failure   I came to understand how touching pop songs

can be and that neither the toyed with
nor the toyers are happy   time always
ran ahead of me and over and over again I had to
pass through a narrow damp space between doors

(Translated by Hye-jin Juhn Sidney & George Sidney)

이제는 다만 때 아닌, 때 늦은 사랑에 대하여

이제는 송곳보다 송곳에 찔린 허벅지에 대하여
말라붙은 눈꺼풀과 문드러진 입술에 대하여
정든 유곽의 맑은 아침과 식은 아랫목에 대하여
이제는, 정든 유곽에서 빠져 나올 수 없는 한 발
자국을
위하여 질퍽이는 눈길과 하품하는 굴뚝과 구정
물에 흐르는
종소리를 위하여 더럽혀진 처녀들과 비명에 간 사
내들의
썩어가는 팔과 꾸들꾸들한 눈동자를 위하여 이
제는
누이들과 처제들의 꿈꾸는, 물 같은 목소리
에 취하여
버려진 조개 껍질의 보라색 무늬와 길바닥에 쓰
러진
까치의 암록색 꼬리에 취하여 노래하리라 정
든 유곽
어느 잔칫집 어느 상갓집에도 찾아다니며 피어
나고
떨어지는 것들의 낮은 신음 소리에 맞추어 녹은 것
구부러진 것 얼어붙은 것 갈라터진 것 나가떨어
진 것들

옆에서 한 번, 한 번만 보고 싶음과 만지고 싶
음과 살 부비고 싶음에
관하여 한 번, 한 번만 부여안고 휘이 돌고 싶
음에 관하여
이제는 다만 때 아닌, 때 늦은 사랑에 관하여

现在只说迟到的爱来得不是时候

现在要说的不是锥子而是被锥子刺中的大腿
是干涸的眼皮和破烂的嘴唇
是日久生情的妓院晴朗的早晨和冷却的炕头
现在为了无法从日久生情的妓院迈出的脚印
为了泥泞的雪路和哈欠连天的烟囱和污水中
流淌的钟声　为了被玷污的处女和死于悲鸣的男子汉们
腐烂的手臂和硬邦邦的眼珠　现在
陶醉于姐姐和小姨子们梦中如水的声音
陶醉于贝壳的紫纹和躺在路上的喜鹊
的暗绿色尾巴　歌唱　在日久生情的妓院
在喜宴人家和丧事人家也绽放和凋落的事物
配合着它们低沉的呻吟而融化的事物
弯曲的　冰冻的　崩裂的　跌落的事物

在旁边看一眼 只看一眼　渴望抚摸　肌肤相亲
抱一次　只抱一次 渴望旋转
现在只说迟到的爱，来得不是时候

Now Only About Love that Came at the Wrong Time, Too Late

Now about a thigh pierced by an awl rather than about the awl
about caked-dry eyelids and disfigured lips   about fresh mornings
in the congenial brothel, and the chill, less-heated side of the room
Now about that one step that can't be taken so as to leave the congenial
brothel   about the slush road, the yawning chimney, and the sound of
a bell that flows along with the muddy water   about despoiled virgins
and the rotting arms and dried-out eyeballs of men who died untimely
Now drunk on the fluid dreamy voices of older sisters
        and younger
sisters-in-law, drunk on the purple pattern of an abandoned seashell,
on the blue-green tail of a dead magpie on the road, I'll sing in tune
with the deep moans of all who go to their congenial brothel, to homes
where there are parties, to homes mourning deaths of all

who blossom
and collapse   about wanting to see you once, just once
more, wanting
to touch you, to mesh our flesh, to be beside what's been
melted, bent,
frozen, split open, hurled aside   about wanting to look at
you once,
just once   and about wanting to hold you and to whirl
around holding you in my arms
Now only about love that came at the wrong time,
too late

(Translated by Hye-jin Juhn Sidney & George Sidney)

序詩

간이식당에서 저녁을 사 먹었습니다
늦고 헐한 저녁이 옵니다
낯선 바람이 부는 거리는 미끄럽습니다
사랑하는 사람이여, 당신이 맞은편 골목에서
문득 나를 알아볼 때까지
나는 정처 없습니다

당신이 문득 나를 알아볼 때까지
나는 정처 없습니다
사방에서 새소리 번쩍이며 흘러내리고
어두워 가며 몸 뒤트는 풀밭,
당신을 부르는 내 목소리
키 큰 미류나무 사이로 잎잎이 춤춥니다

序诗

我在简易餐厅吃晚饭
黄昏来临，轻松而缓慢
陌生的风吹来，街道很滑
我爱的人啊，我无所适从
直到你在对面的巷子里
突然认出我

我无所适从
直到你突然认出我
四周有鸟鸣闪烁和流淌
凌乱的草地越来越暗
我呼唤你的声音
在高大的白杨树间翩翩起舞

Prelude

I ate dinner at a snack bar
evening comes on, laggard and late
an unfamiliar wind slicks smooth the street
My love, until you of a sudden notice me
from where you are across the street
I won't know where I'm going

My love, until you of a sudden notice me
I won't know where I'm going
birds' sounds trill brightly all around
and the grass twists dark in the dusk
My voice, calling you,
dances among the rustling leaves of a tall poplar

(Translated by Hye-jin Juhn Sidney & George Sidney)

세월의 습곡이여, 기억의 단층이여

무엇과도 바꿀 수 없는 날들이 흘러갔다
강이 하늘로 흐를 때,
명절 떡쌀에 햇살이 부서질 때
우리가 아픈 것은 삶이 우리를
사랑하기 때문이다

무엇과도 바꿀 수 없는 날들이 흘러갔다
흐르는 안개가 아마포처럼 몸에 감길 때,
짐 실은 말 뒷다리가 사람 다리보다 아름다울 때
삶이 가엾다면 우린 거기
묶일 수밖에 없다

岁月的褶皱，记忆的断层

任何事物都无法替换的日子流过
河水流向天空的时候
阳光碎在节日打糕米里的时候
我们之所以痛苦　是因为生活
热爱我们

任何事物都无法替换的日子流过
流淌的迷雾像亚麻布一样缠住身体的时候
驮着货物的马的后腿比人腿更美丽的时候
如果觉得生活可怜　那么我们
只能被束缚在那里

The Folding of Time, The Dislocation of Memory

The days we wouldn't trade for anything have flowed by
when the river flows skyward,
when sunbeams are mashed into the rice for the holiday ttok,
the reason we're sick is that
life loves us

The days we wouldn't trade for anything have flowed by
when like linen the flowing fog enwraps our bodies,
when the hind legs of a horse, a load on its back, seem more
beautiful than human legs
Even if we feel sorry for life we have no choice
but to be tied to it

(Translated by Hye-jin Juhn Sidney & George Sidney)

높이 치솟은 소나무 숲이

높이 치솟은 소나무숲이 불안하였다 밤, 하늘의 구름은 층층이 띠를 이루고 그 사이 하늘은 무늬 넣은 떡처럼 쌓였다 층층이, 하늘에 가면 말이 필요할까 이곳은 말이 통하지 않는 곳
이곳은 말이 통하지 않아! 집에 가면 오늘도 아버지 집에 낯선 사람들이 찾아온다 그들은 모두 피를 본 사람들이다 의로운 자들, 스스로 의롭게 여기는 자들의 입에 피가 묻어 있다 의로운 자들의 입에서 피가 웃는다 아버지는 그들을 몹시 사랑하신다
아, 하고 내 입에서 낮은 한숨이 나온다 오늘 밤 그들은 시끄러운 예언자를 묶어 나무에 매달 것이다 예언자도 그리 믿을 만한 사람은 못 된다 그의 배는 부르고 걱정이 없다 아무도 걱정하는 사람은 없고……
소나무 숲은 더욱 불안해진다 달이 소나무 숲으로 밀려가고 물은 움직이지 않는다

高耸的松林

高耸的松林躁动不安　夜晚，天上的云层层相连
　天空像花纹糕点堆积其间　一层层，天空需要
　语言吗　这里语言不通
这里语言不通！回家　今天又有陌生人来找父亲
　他们都是见过血的人　正义者，自以为正义的
　人们嘴角有血　血在正义者的嘴里微笑　父亲
　热爱他们
啊，我低声叹息　今天夜里　他们捆绑多嘴的预言
　家　吊上树枝　预言家也不值得相信　他衣食
　无忧　无所牵挂……
松林更加不安　月亮滑向松林　水静止不动

The Forest of Tall Pine Trees

The forest of tall pine trees was foreboding night, the
clouds stacked up layer upon layer, strips of sky in between
like a layered rice cake will words be necessary in
heaven here words are not understood
Words are not understood here! today at home
strangers again come to visit our father all of them
have spilled blood there is blood on the lips of these
righteous people, of these people who see themselves as
righteous blood grins on the lips of these righteous
people my father loves them very much
Aah, a soft sigh escapes my mouth tonight they are
going to tie up the prating prophet and hang him from
a tree you can't even depend upon a prophet his
stomach's full he has no worries nobody's worried ...
The forest of pine trees looks even more foreboding
the moon's been blown toward the forest, and the water is
still

(Translated by Hye-jin Juhn Sidney & George Sidney)

신기하다, 신기해, 햇빛 찬연한 밤마다

어째서 산은 삼각형인가 어째서 물은 삼각형
　으로 흐르지 않는가 어째서 여자 젖가슴
　은 두 개뿐이고 어미 개의 젖가슴은 여
　덟 개인가 언제부터 젖가슴은 무덤을 닮았
　는가 어떻게 한 나무의 꽃들은 같은 색, 같
　은 무늬를 가졌는가 어째서 달팽이는 딱딱
　한 껍질 속에서 소리지르지 않고 귤껍질
　은 주황색으로 빛나며 풀이 죽는가 귤껍질
　의 슬픔은 어디서 오는가
어째서 병신들은 바로 걷지 못하고 전봇대는 완
　강히 버티고 서 있는가 왜 해가 떠도 밤인
　가 매일 밤 물오리는 어디에서 자는가 무
　슨 수를 써서 조개는 멋진 껍질을 만드는
　가 왜 청년들은 月經을 하지 않는가 어째
　서 동네 깡패들은 의리에 죽고 의리에 사
　는가 왜 장님은 앞을 못 보고 소방서에서
　는 불이 나지 않는가 불에 타 죽어가는 새
　들은 무슨 말을 하는가
왜 술 먹은 사람은 헛소리를 하고 술 안 먹
　은 사람도 헛소리를 하는가 매일 밤 돌사
　자는 무엇을 기다리는가 언제부터 風向計
　는 우두커

니 땅만 내려다보는가 어째서 귀여운 아이들
의 볼그레한 뺨은 썩었는가 누가 소녀들
의 가랑이를 벌리고 말뚝을 박았는가 언제
부터 창녀들은 같은 길 같은 골목에서 서
성거리고 초라한 사내들은 어떻게 알고 찾
아오는가
신기하다, 신기해, 햇빛 찬연한 밤마다 惡夢을 보
내주신 그대,
목마름을 다오! 身熱을 다오!

新奇啊，新奇，每个阳光灿烂的夜晚

山怎么会是三角形　水为什么不以三角形流淌　女人的乳房为什么只有两个　母狗的乳房却有八个　从什么时候开始乳房酷似坟墓　一棵树的花为什么同色同纹　蜗牛为什么躲在硬壳里不吭声　橘子皮萎缩了为什么是橘黄色　橘子皮的悲伤从何而来

瘸子为什么不能正常走路　电线杆为什么顽强挺立　为什么太阳当空却是夜晚　每天夜里鸭子在哪儿睡觉　蛤蜊用什么手段造出漂亮的外壳　为什么小伙子不来月经　村里的混混们为什么生于义气又死于义气　盲人为什么看不见前方　消防署为什么不着火　被火烧死的鸟们说什么

为什么喝酒的人胡说八道　不喝酒的人也胡说八道　每天晚上石狮子在等什么　从什么时候开始风向标只是呆呆地俯视地面　可爱的孩子们红通通的脸蛋为什么

腐烂　谁劈开少女的双腿往里打桩　从什么时候开始妓女在同一条路同一条胡同里徘徊　寒酸的男人们怎么会沿路而来

新奇啊，新奇，每个阳光灿烂的夜晚送来噩梦的你，

赐我以渴！赐我以热！

Amazing, How Amazing It Is, Every Night of the Shining Sun

Why is the shape of a mountain triangular why doesn't
water flow in the shape of a triangle why do women
have only one pair of nipples, and bitches four since
when have breasts been shaped like burial mounds how
is it that a tree's blossoms are all of the same color and
pattern why don't snails rage out against their hard
shells, and why does a tangerine's skin glow golden as it
withers what's the source of its sorrow
Why can't the lame walk normally and why are electric
power poles so obstinately erect why is it night
even after the sun rises where do ducks sleep at
night by what means do mollusks create such ingenious
shells why don't young men menstruate why
do neighborhood thugs live for friendship and die for
friendship why can't the blind see and why isn't there
fire in fire stations what do birds burning to death say
Why do people who drink alcohol and also those who don't
drink alcohol babble nonsense what do statuary stone
lions wait for every night since when do wind vanes do
nothing but stare down at the ground why do the pink
cheeks of cute children decay who spread and rammed a

rod up between the legs of young girls   since when have
whores been hanging out on the same corners of the same
streets and how do their shabby johns know where to look
for them
Amazing, how amazing it is   come, you who sent me
nightmares every night of the shining sun,
give me more thirst! Give my body more fever!

(Translated by Hye-jin Juhn Sidney & George Sidney)

수박

여름날 오후 뜨거운 언덕받이를 타고 아파트
로 가는 길엔 어른이나 아이나 제 머리통
보다 큰 수박 하나씩 비닐끈에 묶어 들
고 땀 흘리며, 땀 닦으며 정신없이 기
어 오른다 그들이 오르막 길에서 허우적거
릴 땐 손에 달린 수박이 떼구르르 구를 것
도 같고, 굴러 내려 쇠뭉치로 만든 공처
럼 땅 속 깊이 묻혀 버릴 것도 같지만 무
사히, 무사히 수박은 개구멍 같은 아파
트 현관 속으로 들어간다

그럼 이제 어떤 일이 벌어지는가 우선 끈에 묶
인 수박을 풀고 간단히 씻은 다음, 검은 등
에 흰 배의 고등어 같은 부엌칼로 띵띵 부
은 수박의 배를 가르면, 끈적거리는 단물
을 흘리며 벌겋게 익은 속이 쩍, 갈라 떨어
지고 쥐똥 같은 검은 알이 튀어 나온다 그
러면 저마다 스텐 숟가락을 손에 쥔 아버
지와 할머니, 큰아이와 작은놈, 머리를 뒤
로 묶은 딸아이가 달겨들어 파먹기 시작하
고, 언제나 뒷처리하는 어머니는 이따금 숟
가락 집어 거들기도 하지만, 어머니는 입맛
이 없다

어느새 수박씨는 마루 여기저기 흩어지고 허
연 뱃대기를 드러낸 수박 껍데기가 깨
진 사기 접시처럼 쌓일 때, 아이들은 자
리를 박차고 뛰쳐 나가고 할머니는 건넌
방에 드러눕고 아버지는 값싼 담배를 붙
여 물고, 게으르고 긴 연기를 뿜을 것이다
그것은 어느 여름 어른들이 겪었다던 물난리 같
은 것일까 질퍽하고 구질구질한 난장판 같
은 것일까 아버지의 작업복을 기워 만
든 걸레로 마루바닥을 훔치며 어머니는 바
닥 여기저기 묻어 있는 수박물을 볼 것이
다 벌건, 그러나 약간은 어둡고 끈끈한 수
박물을...... 왠지 쓸쓸해지기만 하는 어
떤 삶을......

西瓜

夏日午后　沿着炙热的坡顶去公寓的路上　大人和孩子
都用塑料绳提着比自己脑袋还大的西瓜　流汗　擦汗
努力往上爬　他们在上坡路苦苦挣扎　提在手里的西
瓜好像要滚落　像铁球深埋在地里　结果安然无恙
西瓜安然无恙　安然无恙地进入狗洞般的公寓门

那么　现在会有什么事吗　首先放下绳子捆住的西瓜
简单清洗　再用黑背白腹的鲐鱼似的菜刀切开圆滚滚
的西瓜　流着黏稠的甜水　流出熟透的红瓤　溅出老
鼠屎样的黑籽　手握不锈钢勺子的父亲　祖母　大儿
子和小儿子　头发扎在后面的女儿跑来　狼吞虎咽
总做善后的母亲偶尔拿起勺子　但是母亲没有胃口

转眼间　地板上到处都是西瓜子　露着白肚皮的西瓜皮
像破碎的瓷盘堆积起来　孩子们起身跑出了门　祖母
到隔壁躺下　父亲点燃廉价香烟叼在嘴里　准备吐出
慵懒而悠长的烟雾

像某年夏天大人们经历的水灾？还是泥泞而污秽的混
乱？母亲用父亲的工作服改成的抹布擦地板看见满地
的西瓜汁　红色的稍微黑暗和黏稠的西瓜汁……怎么
有点儿像是凄凉的人生……

Watermelon

One summer afternoon on the hillside path up to the
apartment block   families, children as well as adults
toil upward, sweating, wiping away the sweat, each
lugging a plastic twine-netted watermelon larger than
their heads   as they grab at the air for balance it seems
that the melons dangling from their hands will go rolling
down the hill and like balls of iron bury themselves at the
bottom   but the melons make their way safely, safely into
the cubbyhole entrance of the building
Now what happens   the members of a family first undo
the twine   they wash the melon and with a kitchen knife
resembling a black-backed, white-bellied mackerel they
split open the swollen-to-bursting stomach   sweet sticky
juice seeps from the ripe red insides, and black seeds like
rat droppings pop out   then the father, the grandmother,
the first son, the second son, the pony-tailed daughter, each
wielding a stainless steel spoon fall upon the melon and dig
into it   the mother, who always finishes off whatever
scraps remain, from time to time lifts her spoon and joins
them, but without much appetite
Finally, seeds strewn all about and pieces of naked white
belly-rind stacked up like porcelain dishes, the children dash

outside the grandmother lies down in her room   the father lights a cheap cigarette and blows out long lazy streams of smoke
Is this similar to that calamitous flood the older people tell us they lived through one summer   is it similar to that turbid squalid mess wiping the floor with a rag she'd made from the father's old work clothes the mother comes upon watermelon juice that's dribbled down here and there upon the floor, watermelon juice, red, dark red, sticky ... a life of deepening loneliness ...

(Translated by Hye-jin Juhn Sidney & George Sidney)

남해 금산

한 여자 돌 속에 묻혀 있었네
그 여자 사랑에 나도 돌 속에 들어갔네
어느 여름 비 많이 오고
그 여자 울면서 돌 속에서 떠나갔네
떠나가는 그 여자 해와 달이 끌어주었네
남해 금산 푸른 하늘가에 나 혼자 있네
남해 금산 푸른 바닷물 속에 나 혼자 잠기네

南海锦山

一个女人被埋进了石头。
因为爱她我也走进了石头
有一年夏天雨水很多
那个女人哭着从石头里离开
太阳和月亮指引着离去的女人
我独自守着南海锦山蔚蓝的天边
我独自潜入南海锦山蔚蓝的海水

South Sea, Silk Mountain

A woman was immured in stone
for her love I followed her into the stone
One summer it rained a lot
weeping, she left the stone
led by sun and moon she left
I'm alone now at the edge of the blue sky above Silk
Mountain by the South Sea
alone I sink into the blue water of the South Sea at
Silk Mountain

(Translated by Hye-jin Juhn Sidney & George Sidney)

作者简介

李晟馥，生于1952年，诗作极富想象力，层次丰富，一向备受瞩目，曾荣获金洙暎文学奖及素月诗歌文学奖。李晟馥深受卡夫卡、尼采及波德莱尔影响，首部诗集《滚石何时醒来》中诗人充当临床病理学家，剖析家庭和社会结构，并仔细记录其逐渐瓦解的过程，联想奔放大胆，戳破世界的虚伪、腐败及堕落，深深震撼读者。李晟馥的第二本诗集《南海锦山》源于他对东亚古典文学的兴趣，作品中多有对爱的本质的探讨。他其后的诗集中一直延续着这个主题，为“爱”另造新语法，反映现代人的情爱观念。诗人同时不断求新，倡导诗歌改革，影响了不少同代和年轻一代的诗人。

评论家金玹指出李晟馥的诗作“大大扩展意义的领域，启迪无尽的问题，问题不单局限于个人或私人层面，甚至扩展至集体及公众的层面”。李晟馥的诗作不断游走于两个层面，展现人生底蕴中的基本关系。

李晟馥于首尔大学取得法国文学学士及硕士学位，曾任启明大学法国文学系及创意写作系教授。主要著作包括《滚石何时醒来》（1980）、《南海锦山》（1986）、《那年夏末》（1990）、《虎狼加时树的回忆》（1993）、《啊，没有嘴巴的东西！》（2003）、《月儿前额的波浪纹》（2003）、《来，看看悲伤就是全部》（2013）等。

（谢小婷译）

Lee Seong-bok (1952–   ), recipient of Kim Soo-young Literature Prize and Kim So-wol Literature Prize, has continually attracted attention to his highly imaginative and multi-layered poetry. Influenced by Kafka, Nietzsche and Baudelaire, Lee's first volume of poetry *When Do the Rolling Stones Awake* shocked readers with its daring use of free association to expose the hypocrisy, corruption and perversity of this world. In this volume, the poet occupies the place of a clinical pathologist who dissects familial and social structures, and meticulously records their gradual disintegration. His second book *Mt. Geum, Nahmae*, shaped by the poet's new interest in the East Asian classical literature, largely deals with the question of love's essence. The subject continues to engross Lee in subsequent volumes as well, and he creates an alternative grammar of love to the modern notion of romance. Driven by a spirit of innovation, Lee heralds a poetic revolution that influences both his contemporaries and younger generation of poets. The critic Kim Hyoun has said of Lee Seong-bok's poetry that "it vastly expands its sphere of meaning to permit endless questions to be raised, not only on an individual or private level, but on the collective and public one as well." Moving unceasingly between binary categories, Lee's poetry thus brings into view the fundamental relation that lies beneath human life.

Lee earned both his undergraduate and graduate degrees in French literature from the Seoul National University. He worked as Professor of French literature and creative writing at the Keimyung University.

His major works include *When Do the Rolling Stones Awake* (1980), *South Sea, Silk Mountain* (1986), *End of That Summer* (1990), *Memories of the Holly* (1993), *Oh, Those without Mouths* (2003), *Ripple Patterns on the Moon's Forehead* (2003), *Came, and Saw Sorrow Was All* (2013).

图书在版编目（CIP）数据

新奇啊，新奇，每个阳光灿烂的夜晚：朝、汉、英 /(韩) 李晟馥著；薛舟，谢小婷译. -- 南京：江苏凤凰文艺出版社，2021.1

（红狐丛书. 一衣带水的相望）

ISBN 978-7-5594-1387-1

Ⅰ. ①新… Ⅱ. ①李… ②薛… ③谢… Ⅲ. ①诗集－韩国－现代－朝鲜语、汉语、英语 Ⅳ. ①I312.625

中国版本图书馆CIP数据核字(2019)第160951号

红狐丛书·一衣带水的相望：新奇啊，新奇，每个阳光灿烂的夜晚

北岛 主编
（韩）李晟馥 著
薛舟 谢小婷 译

出 版 人　张在健
责任编辑　王娱瑶　于奎潮
特约编辑　薛　倩　傅春晖
书籍设计　周伟伟
责任印制　刘　巍
出版发行　江苏凤凰文艺出版社
　　　　　南京市中央路165号，邮编：210009
出版社网址　http://www.jswenyi.com
印　　刷　苏州越洋印刷有限公司
开　　本　880×1230毫米　1/32
印　　张　3.625
字　　数　37千字
版　　次　2021年1月第1版
印　　次　2021年1月第1次印刷
标准书号　ISBN 978-7-5594-1387-1
定　　价　128.00元（全七册）

红狐丛书·东亚卷 | 北岛 主编

A Poem for A Book

ein gedicht fuer ein Buch

一诗一书

Yoko Tawada

［日］多和田叶子 著 田原 毛乙馨 方太初 译

江苏凤凰文艺出版社
JIANGSU PHOENIX LITERATURE AND ART PUBLISHING

目录

Contents

A Poem for A Book

Yoko Tawada

線から生まれた人々

1. 人

「人」という字は貧弱に見える
脳味噌もないし、靴も履いてない
手があれば火を起こすことができるだろうに
明るさも暖かさも自分ではつくりだせない
何もできない人にできることは何か
砂浜に立って海をみつめること
因幡の白兎みたいに
鰐に皮を剥がれるかもしれない
火あぶり用の薪の山に投げ込まれるかもしれない
社会はたえず生け贄を捜している
肉が焼ける時に出るエネルギーはクリーンで自然なエネルギーなんだそうだ

「人」という字は歩いているように見えるか
それとも立ち止まっているように見えるか

2. 木

「丁」の字は、背骨の延長線が上空に向かってまっすぐ延びていき　いつか雲の柔らかさにぶつかって
もうそれ以上　昇らなくてもいいね

と思える　その瞬間をあらわす
そうして人が木になる
瘤だらけで背骨の曲がった梅の木
植物は哺乳類が発達した形だそうだ
光と水と二酸化炭素だけから　色と形の文化を作る
無駄な物は食べないので　くさい排泄物を腸からひねり
　　出さなくても生きていける
家を建てる代わりに自分の身体を
毛虫にキツツキに栗鼠に家として与える

3. 水

天に昇るのがパイロットの仕事ならば
天から落ちるのが天使の仕事
雲の編み目から落ちてくる落ちてくる
水もしたたるいい天使たち
濡れて鏡になった高速道路に
肩を叩きつけられ
くだけて飛沫になる
道路は水滴を集めて先を急ぐ川になり
川はやがて大蛇になり
うねりくねり　人の住む地の岸を削り取り

土砂を運び
地球の顔を彫り上げていく

4. 米

茶碗いっぱいに星が盛りつけてある
とがった光の先端が
米食う人の舌を甘く刺すと
眼球の裏側にさわやかな風が流れこむ
さっきまで壁のよごれだと思っていたのは七匹の蚊その脚にはえた産毛まではっきり見える
星米を食べると遠くが見えるのだそうだ
三十キロ先の海辺で幼な児が鼻血をたらしながら蟹と遊んでいるのが見える
三年先に無人銀行の窓が風にあおられてバタンバタンと開いたり閉まったりしているのが見える

5. 犬

男が一人　崖っぷちにしゃがんで
お皿みたいに平らな犬の頭を左手で撫でている
右手を差し出して犬にやさしく噛ませ
涎に濡れた手の甲を見つめ

犬の首から首輪をはずして代わりに花輪をかけ
いきなり抱きしめて
犬の目に自分の頬を押しつけ
涙を浮かべて
犬の頭を両腕できつく抱きしめ
それから
溶岩のぐつぐつ煮える活火山口に　犬を突き落とした

6. 大

「美」とは大きな羊のことらしい
生け贄が大きければ禍は小さくなるらしい
大きな傘は弱い風にあおられただけで　すぐに骨が曲がってしまう
強制収容所では背の高い人から順番に亡くなっていったらしい
大きな人は小さな人を食べる
大きな国は小さな国が嫌いだ
大きな鼠は小さな象を尊敬する

7. 太

夜明けと夕闇が溶け合い
暑さと寒さが同じ意味になる時代が来る
ゆっくり歩くと駅は近く感じられ
おせんべいを一枚食べただけでもう満腹で
もう書くのはやめようと思った詩がいつの間にか紙の上
　に姿を現す

8. 未

まだ死んでない人とは今話をすることができる
まだ触ったことのない自分の腹の中、内臓
まだ逢ったことのない人がまだ訪れてない悲しみに打
ちひしがれたわたしを慰めてくれる
その時使われる言語をわたしはまだ学習し始めていない
まだ書かれてない詩は常にすでに書かれている
まだ想像することもできないくらいずっと先にある地球
　の未来では人間以外の生き物たちがもっと幸せに
　なっているといい

9. 末

袖の末には繊細な手がある
裾の末にはしなやかで力強い足首がある

思考の末には呼吸がある
わたしは
片足を鶴のようにもちあげ
扇を持った右手を翼のように開いて
人から鳥へ
鳥から文字へと変化していく

10. 来

あなたの立っている場所が分からない
それはわたしが昔立っていたところ？
戻って来いという声が聞こえるけれど
まだ行ったことのないところにしか戻りたくない

自线而生的人们

1. 人

“人”这个字看上去很贫弱
既没大脑，也没穿鞋
如果有手，也许能生火
但却无法创造光明和温暖
一事无成的人究竟能干吗
站在沙滩眺望大海
如同因幡的白兔[1]
或许会被鳄鱼剥了皮
或被当作木柴扔进火堆
人类社会在不停搜寻祭品
据说肉被烧烤时产生的能源既无污染又很天然

“人”这个字看上去像在行走吗？
还是像一动不动地站着？

2. 木

“丁”字是沿着脊柱的延长线笔直向天伸展，
直到撞上云的柔软
到此为止，不再上升也可以吧

在这个想法出现的瞬间
于是，人变成木
脊柱弯曲满身疙瘩的梅树
据说植物是哺乳动物的进化形态
只靠光、水和二氧化碳，创造颜色和形状的文化
由于不食多余之物，即使不从肠子挤出恶臭的排泄物也照样能活
取代自己造房的是，用自己的身体
为毛毛虫、啄木鸟和松鼠提供归宿

3. 水

如果登天是飞行员的工作
那么自天而降便是天使的本职
从云的针眼落下、落下
滴着水珠可爱的天使们
在淋湿成镜子的高速公路上
被拍了一下肩膀
就碎成了飞溅的泡沫
公路匆匆地积水成河
不久河变成巨蛇
潮涨潮落，吞噬人类的居所之岸

搬运砂土
去雕刻地球的面孔

4. 米
盛上满满一碗星星
尖锐的光线头部
温柔地刺向食米者的舌头
眼球内部清爽的风流动
刚刚还以为是墙上的污垢，现在连那七只蚊子脚
　上长出的细毛都能看清
好像吃了星米就能看清远方
看得见三十公里外的海边，淌着鼻血的小孩捉蟹玩儿
看得见三年前无人的银行之窗被风吹得咣当咣当
　时开时合

5. 犬
一个男人，蹲在悬崖边
左手摸着平如盘底的狗头
伸出右手让狗轻轻啃咬
盯着被狗的口水弄湿的手心

从狗的头上摘下颈圈，戴上花环
突然将它抱住
往狗眼上贴紧自己的脸颊
热泪盈眶
用两条手臂死死地抱紧狗的头
然后
在翻滚着熔岩的活火山口，把狗推了下去

6. 大
“美”这个字仿佛一只很大的羊
据说祭品越大灾祸越小
大伞被微风轻拂，马上就折弯了腰
据说在强制收容所里，从个子高的人开始逐个死亡
体格大的人吃掉体格小的
国土大的嫌弃国土小的
大的老鼠尊敬小的象

7. 太

黎明与黄昏融合在一起
酷暑与寒冷变成同一个意思的时代到来
慢慢走会感觉车站很近
只吃一块脆饼就已很饱
已决定不再写的诗却不觉间出现在纸上

8. 未

还未死的人现在还能说话
未曾触摸过的是自己的腹中和内脏
素不相识的人安慰被仍未到来的悲伤击垮的我
我还未开始学习那时使用的语言
未完成的诗常常已被写出
未能想象的遥远未来，地球上人类之外的生物能
　活得更幸福该有多好

9. 末

袖口的末端有纤细的手
裤管的末端有敏捷且有力的脚踝

思考的末端有呼吸
我像单脚站立的鹤，用手举起
像握着扇子的右手展开翅膀
从人到鸟
从鸟到文字的演变

10. 来
不知你站在何方
难道那是我曾经站过的地方？
虽然传来“快回来”的召唤声
却只想回到从未去过的地方

译注：

1 因幡的白兔引自日本《古事记》出云神话，讲述了想要渡河前往因幡国的兔子，在隐岐岛针对鳄鱼想了条诡计，以比一比素菟族还是鳄族的数量多为由，而使鳄鱼从隐岐岛排队到了因幡国。踩在鳄鱼背上渡河的白兔在眼看计划就要成功之际，嘲笑鳄鱼愚笨，于是被鳄鱼剥了皮。

People Born of Lines

1. Person[1]

The character for "person" looks so sparse
No brain, no shoes to wear
If it just had hands, it could light a fire
But it cannot create light or warmth on its own
What can a person who does nothing do?
Stand on the sand and gaze at the sea
Like the white rabbit at Inaba[2]
His skin might be torn off by a crocodile
He might be thrown on a pile of firewood to be
burned at the stake
Society seeks an unending supply of human sacrifices
They say the energy released as a body burns is green
    and natural

Does the character for "person" look like it is walking
Or does it seem to stand transfixed?

2. Trees

The character （丁） stretches straight up the length
    of its spine
At some point it will strike the softness of the clouds

It shows the moment it thinks
There is no need to go any higher
And then people become trees
Plum trees with crooked spines and covered in bumps
They say plants are in mammalian forms
They make cultures of color and form from only
    light, water, and carbon dioxide
They do not eat unnecessarily, that is the reason they can live
Without excreting foul-smelling waste from their entrails
Instead of building houses, they give their own
    bodies as homes
To the caterpillars, to the woodpeckers, to the squirrels

3. Water

If ascending to the heavens is the job of a pilot
Then falling from the heavens is the job of an angel
Water too is a band of good angels
That falls and falls from the stitches of the clouds
Stuck on the shoulder, they pelt down
Onto the wet mirror of the highway
And smash into spray
The road collects the drops and becomes a rushing river

Which eventually becomes a large serpent
That twists and turns, carving away the shores of people's land
Carrying earth and sand
It carves away, leaving the face of the earth in relief

4. Rice

A pile of stars fills her bowl
The tips of the sharp ray of light
Sweetly sting the mouth of the ones who eat it
A refreshing breeze flows in behind their eyes
What looked like spot on the wall is now seven
mosquitoes, the hair of their legs clearly visible
They say eating star-rice allows one to see into the distance
Thirty kilometers away, a small child is visible, nose
bleeding, as it plays with a crab
Three years away, the window of an unmanned bank is
visible as it blows in the wind, banging open and shut

5. Dog

A single man squats on the precipice
His left hand rubs the head of his dog, flat as a plate
He sticks out his right hand and lets it gently bite

He gazes at his palm, slick with saliva

Takes off the dog's collar, replaces it with a chain of flowers

Suddenly embraces it

Presses his cheek against the dog's eyes

The tears well up

He embraces the dog's head firmly with both arms

And then

Pushes the dog into the bubbling lava of the volcano below

6. Large

They say the character "beauty" (美) means "large

(大) sheep (羊)"

They say the larger the living sacrifice, the less the misfortune

Even a small wind will soon bend the spokes of a big umbrella

They say that in prison people die in the order of their height

Big people eat small people

Big countries hate small countries

Big mice respect small elephants

7. Thick

A time will come when dawn will melt into dusk

Warmth will mean the same as cold

Walk slowly and the station will feel nearer
A single cracker will fill our stomachs
And at the moment one wants to stop writing, a
poem appears on the page

8. Not Yet

It is still possible to speak now to those not yet dead
Inside my stomach are entrails I have still not touched
Someone I have not yet met consoles me for a
    crushing sorrow I have not yet felt
The language I use at that moment is one I have not
    yet started to learn
The poems I have not yet written are already written
I hope that the other creatures that I cannot yet
    imagine that will inhabit the earth far into the
    future will be far happier than us

9. End

At the end of the sleeve is a sensitive hand
At the end of the hem is a delicate yet strong ankle
At the end of thought is breath
I raise one foot

Like a crane

I spread out my right hand holding a fan

Like a wing

And I transform from human into a bird

From bird to a letter

10. Come

I do not know where you stand

Is it the place where I once stood long ago?

I hear a voice calling me

But I want to return only to places I have never been

(Translated by Jeffrey Angels)

Translator's Note:

1 Each poem in this sequence has a single Sino-Japanese character or kanji for its title. The shapes of the characters provide the rationale for the sequence of the poems. For instance, the character "people" (人) can be transformed into the character for "trees" (木), with the addition of a couple of strokes, which in turn looks similar to the character for "water" (水), and so on.

2 White rabbit at Inaba: According to an ancient Japanese legend, a white rabbit wanted to cross from Oki Island to the shore of Inaba, so he called upon a wani and challenged him to see whose family was biggest. Pretending to want to count the members of its family, he had the wani line up its family members from one shore to the other, then he bounded across their backs. The wani took revenge for the rabbit's trickery by flaying him with their teeth. The word wani means "crocodile" in modern Japanese, but in the ancient texts, the same word was used to mean "shark."

Einladung zur Boston Tea Party

Als Indianer verkleidet
warf ich die Teekisten in den Atlantik
Welke Blätter öffnen sich wieder im Salzwasser
Die ungemütlichste Teezeremonie
im letzten Jahrtausend
Ich will nicht mehr gesteuert werden,
sagte das Segelschiff, das sich in eine sperrige Insel
verwandelt hatte
Nicht abwarten, nichts trinken
Dreihundertzweiundvierzig Sprünge
ins Fruchtwasser der Großmutter
Der Tag der Ankunft liegt nicht weit zurück
Damals zeichnete ich noch dreieckige Wellen in die Weltkarte
Dazu noch Möwen und ein Monster mit Fischgesicht
Jetzt ist nur noch eine zittrige Linie übrig
Territorien auf der Torte der Terroristen
Unabhängigkeit
lohnt sich nicht
Ein amerikanisches Lexikon beginnt mit A und endet auf A

Zwischen einem Anfang und einem noch früheren Anfang
Zwischen einem Apfel der Sünde und einem Apfel
des Computers
liegt meine Heiterkeit
Ich habe ein Waisenkind britisch gebeizt
Unterwegs, aus Langeweile
Dann bekam ich Fieber
in der nasskalten Maiblume
Der Vordermast hält die ungeduldigen Passagiere zusammen
In einer Kabine findet jede Nacht eine
Transplantation der Stimme statt
Wir vermehren uns, damit wir wieder töten können
Möwen lachen uns aus und legen ihre Plastik-Eier
zwischen zwei
Wellen
Im Schlaf bin ich noch einmal eingeschlafen
Die Dämmerung zieht sich in die feuchte Bettkante zurück

Welche Meerjungfrau ist noch nicht habilitiert?
Bald stürzt der Himmel ab
Der Programmfehler Nummer Zwei: ein nächtlicher Fall
Ich höre ein Raumschiff schluchzen
Zum Glück ist sein Rumpf weich und winzig,
in diesem selbstironischen Kosmos
Unsterblich viele Sternzeichen verraten ihren Chef
und ertrinken zwischen Korallen
Ich fange noch einmal an, beim Buchstaben A
Mit wunden Fingern und dennoch neugierig
Worte brechen, blasen
lallen und Lippen umkippen lassen
Meine Lüge hat zehn Beine
Sie sind kurz aber wasserfest
Ich bin aus einer Zellenprobe geboren
habe keine Eltern zu töten
Ein Foto aus der Kindheit:
Ein Segelschiff, das seine Wurzeln in den Ozean schlägt
Ein Schiff war früher ein Postbote, eine Bibliothek,
ein Krankenhaus, eine Schule, ein Kühlschrank

Ein Schiff war ein Telefon
Auf dem Deck Stimmbänder der Fremden
Was hier vibriert, wird woanders zur Sprache
Eine Zahl wählen
magisch verbindet sie
Es läutet
Es unterbricht
Es gleitet hinüber
rasch fliegt es
ist namenlos
Es fährt in ein
Nicht-Wort
Der Wind stand mir gegenüber
ohne einen Plan, genau gefahren
vielleicht rückwärts
Weiter wie eine Windhose
Alles was duftet und rauscht
aufzählen und sammeln
Für den Tag der Feierlichkeit
Eine Liste der Bewunderungen aufstellen:

1. Klare Architektur trinken
2. Lampen lieben
3. Nicht zurückziehen
4. Einen böhmischen Witz verstehen
5. Nicht immer mitessen
6. Handfläche warm halten
7. Jemanden spontan umarmen können
8. Nur das Extreme aussprechen
9. E-Mail süchtig sein
10. Kleine, gebundene Notizbücher dabei haben
11. Jede Linie verfeinern und dabei immer größere Bogen zeichnen

获邀去波士顿茶会

伪装成印第安人
我把茶叶箱子抛进大西洋
萎靡的叶身在海水中再盛放
令人不安的茶道
在上一个千禧年
帆船说，我不欲被控制
并转化成了巨大的岛
不等待，不喝酒
三百四十二跳
跳进祖母的羊水
抵达之期不是太久以前
其时我甚至在世界地图上画下三角波
加上海鸥及一只长着鱼脸的怪物
现在只余一条摇晃不定的线
恐怖分子的蛋糕领土
独立
并不值得呢
一本美国辞典从 A 开始到 A 结束
在一个开端与更早的开端之间
在一个有罪的苹果与屏幕里的苹果之间
正是我的乐趣

我已弄污了一个孤儿英国
在路上，出于无聊
然后我发烧了
在潮湿的五月花号
前桅让不耐烦的乘客挤在一起
在船舱里每晚都有迁徙之音取代
我们倍数增加，因而可再杀人
海鸥取笑我们并从塑料两翼下蛋
在昏睡中我又入睡了
暮光归到濡湿的床沿
哪条美人鱼尚未学袍加身？
天空快速瓦解
程序错误二：一次晚间摔倒
我听到宇宙飞船抽泣
幸运的是它的船体软而小
在这自嘲的宇宙里
许多不灭的星丛背叛它们的首领
在珊瑚间溺死
我重新开始，从字母A
以酸痛却好奇的手指
字词爆喷而出

胡言乱语嘴唇翻侧
我的谎言有十条腿
它们短小而防水
我从一个细胞样本里诞
生无父母可弑杀
一张童年照片
一艘帆船，植根于海洋
一只曾是邮差、图书馆、医院、学校、冰箱的船
一只曾是电话的船
异乡人在甲板上的声带
振动着的将在某地变为语言
选择一个号码
奇迹般地连结起来
它有所倾诉
它被干扰
它流逝
那迅速起飞的
无以名状
它进入一种
非有之字
风总袭向我脸

毫无计划，时而离去
有时或倒退
持续如龙卷风
一切发出气味与噪音
列举及召集
为了那庄严的一天
一张令人钦羡的名单展开了：
1. 饮用清晰的建筑物
2. 爱好灯具
3. 切勿退却
4. 了解一个波希米亚笑话
5. 切勿总是一起进餐
6. 保持掌心温热
7. 可以自发拥抱他人
8. 只说极端的话
9. 对电邮上瘾
10. 有数本装帧过的小笔记簿
11. 以精致的线条绘制出更宽阔的曲线

Boston Tea Party

Disguised as an Indian
I threw the crates into the Atlantic
Withered leaves unfolded in the salt water
The most disagreeable tea ceremony
of the last millennium
I don't want to be steered any longer,
said the ship that had become an unwieldy island
No more waiting, no more drinking
Three hundred and forty two leaps
into Grandmother's amniotic fluid
Arrival day wasn't so long ago
I was still drawing triangular waves on the map
along with seagulls and a fish-faced monster
All that's left now is a jittery line
Territories upon the tart of the terrorists
Independence
is overrated
An American dictionary begins with A and ends on A
Between a beginning and an even older beginning
Between the apple of sin and a computer apple
That's the source of my merriment
I tinted an orphan British

on the journey, out of boredom
Then I got a fever
in the cold wet bloom of May
The foremast unites the impatient passengers
In one cabin a voice transplantation occurs nightly
We are increasing in number to be able to kill
Seagulls laugh at us and lay their plastic eggs between
two waves
Sleeping, I fell asleep again
Dawn retreats to the edge of the damp bed
Which mermaid still lacks a graduate degree?
Soon the sky will fall
The second error on the program: a nocturnal collapse
I hear a spaceship sobbing
Its hull, luckily, is small and soft
In this self-ironic cosmos
Immortally many signs of the zodiac betray their boss
and drown amid the coral
Again I begin, with the letter A
Sore-fingered but full of curiosity
Words crack, bubble
babble and turn lips inside out

My lie has ten legs
They are short but water-resistant
An experimental cell gave birth to me
I've no parents to kill
A childhood photograph:
A ship puts down roots in the ocean
A ship was once a mailman, a library, a hospital, a
        school, a refrigerator
A ship was once a telephone
On the deck, foreign vocal cords
Vibrations here become speech in other places
Pick a number
It will magically connect
Ringing
Interruption
Something gliding toward us
Swiftly it flutters
It is nameless
It flies in a
not-word
The wind stood across from me
without any plan, after travelling on course

perhaps backwards
then like a vortex
Catalog and collect
everything fragrant and rustling
for the day of the festivities
Compose a list of admirations:
1. Drinking clear architecture
2. Adoring lamps
3. Never recoiling
4. Understanding jokes from Bohemia
5. Not always joining in a meal
6. Keeping the palms of one's hands warm
7. Being able to embrace someone spontaneously
8. Stating only the extreme
9. Being addicted to e-mail
10. Carrying around little bound notebooks
11. Refining every line while sketching out wilder
and wilder curves

(Translated by Susan Bernofsky)

Ich wollte keine Brücke schlagen

Der Ausdruck, eine Brücke schlagen, erschreckt mich. Das Ufer, auf dem ich stehe, wird plötzlich zu einer Hand, die eine gegen das andere Ufer gerichtete Keule hält. Dieses wird dadurch zu einer Bindung gezwungen. Die Bindung erinnert mich an einen Bindestrich. Deutsch-Französisch. Er ist kein Zauberstab, mit dem man das erste und das zweite Wort in ein drittes verwandeln kann.

Wenn ich mit mir selbst rede, tritt versehentlich ein Buchstabe an die Stelle eines anderen. Eine Brücke oder eine Blücke? Weil die Zunge zu weich ist, hört sich das Wort anders an, als es aussieht. Wie sieht ein Wort überhaupt aus? Es gleicht einer Lücke unter einer Brücke. Unter der Brücke schläft der Fluß in Bewegung. Dort treffe ich Menschen und frage sie: Wollen wir uns ans Ufer setzen und eine Lücke ins Wörterbuch schlagen? Wollen wir eine Lücke aufschlagen wie ein Buch? Oder wollen wir einen schwimmenden Weg bauen?

Die Bilder, die wir von derselben Lücke malen, sind verschieden. Einer schwimmt im Wasser, ein zweiter baut ein Boot und ein dritter sitzt am Ufer und wartet auf Regen. Wer kann einen Blick werfen, der die Form eines Bogens hat? Brücken aus Blickbogen erreichen vielleicht das andere Ufer.

Die Finger des Wassers berühren alles, was in die Nähe kommt: Sommerluft, Zigarettenkippen, Fische und die Erde am Ufer. Die Erde hat keine Angst vor dem Wasser. In dieser Stille wird kein Element durch eine Berührung gelöscht. Das Wasser wird uns finden. Und die Sprache des Windes? Der Klang des Lichtes? Auch sie werden uns finden.

我不想起一座桥

起一座桥的说法，使我惊惧。我站着的那座海岸突然变成一只手，持着指向彼岸的定向仪。由是这些都不由自主地连结起来。这纽带使我想起连接号。德语—法语。并没有魔棒使人将第一与第二字变成另一词。

当我自言自语，字符不经意间错位。此桥还是彼桥？舌头太软，言语听上去不如其是。太初有字，字是什么？就如桥下缝隙。桥下有河流动且沉睡。在那儿，我遇到一些人，并向他们发问：我们想就此坐在岸边，并拉近字典里的间隙？要像打开一本书般打开空隙？还是要建立一条浮途？

从同样的空白中我们画出不一样的图像。有的在水中游，有的在建船，还有一个坐在岸上等降雨。谁能抛出一条弓状的视线呢？弓状的视线或许才能搭桥到达彼岸。

流水的手接触一切，那些近处的都来了：夏风、烟头、鱼和岸边的土地。地球对大水无惧。在此种静默中，没有任何事物可以通过触摸被消除。水会找到我们。风的语言？光的声音？他们也会寻到我们的。

I Didn’t Want to Bridge Anything

The expression “to bridge something” shocks me. The bank on which I stand suddenly becomes a hand that holds a club pointed at the other bank. Through that, it is forced into a bond. The bond reminds me of a hyphen. German-French. It’s not a magic wand with which you can transform the first and second words into a third.

When I talk to myself, a letter accidentally walks into the place of another. A bridge or a blidge? Because the tongue is so soft, the word sounds different from how it looks. What does a word look like anyway? It resembles a blank under a bridge. Under the bridge the river sleeps in motion. I meet people there and ask them: Do you want to sit on the bank and hit blanks into the dictionary? Do you want to open a blank like a book? Or do you want to build a floating path?

The pictures that we paint from the same blanks are different. One swims into the water, a second builds a boat, and a third sits on the bank and waits for rain. Who can throw a glance that has the shape of an arch? Bridges from glance-arches might reach the other bank.

The water's finger touches everything that comes near: Summer air, cigarette butts, fish, and the earth on the bank. The earth has no fear of the water. In this stillness nothing will be extinguish by a touch. The water will find us. And the language of the wind? The sound of the light? They too will find us.

(Translated by Emily Sullivan)

Der Hafenpilz

Lachsforellen
die sich unter der Brücke versammeln
um das Feuerwerk
zu erblicken
Ich habe keine Augen
sagt die eine
Bei mir wächst ein Blumenkohl aus dem Kopf
sagt eine andere und
spannt im Wasser ihren Regenschirm auf
(Am Himmel brennen sie Blumen zu Kohle)
Bald fangen die Feuerblätter an
tief im Bierglas zu tanzen
Dann ist es zu spät
Die Lachsforellen schwimmen zurück in die
Konservenfabrik
ohne Eintritt zu zahlen

海港蘑菇

鳟鱼
在桥下聚集去看那
烟花盛放
一只鱼说　我没有眼睛
另一只鱼说
我头上长出了一颗菜花
并在水里张开她的伞
（夜幕下已开成荼蘼花事了）
顷刻火树银花
舞于啤酒瓶底
为时已晚了
鳟鱼洄游罐头工场
无需支付入场费

The Harbor Mushroom

Salmon trout
that assemble under the bridge
to catch a glimpse
of the fireworks
I have no eyes
says one
A cauliflower is growing out of my head
says another and
opens up its umbrella in the water
(On the sky they are burning flowers into coal)
Soon the fire-leaves begin
to dance deep in the beer glass
Then it is too late
the salmon trout swim back
into the canning factory
without paying for entrance

(Translated by Emily Sullivan)

Ein Gedicht fuer Ein Buch

ein wort
ein mord
wenn ich spreche
bin ich nicht da
ein wort
in seinem käfig
fesselnd gefesselt
spuckt einen bericht
über meine taten
über meine karten
kein wort
nur sein schatten
in dem ich ruhe
mein schatten verschwindet darin
nichts wird bewertet
wenn ich schweige
bin ich aus demselben stoff gemacht
wie du
stoffliche zeit
zwischen einem wort

und einem schluck wasser
dort
wo die stimme im fleisch aufwacht
hört man ohne ohren
ein wort
befreit von seinem dienst
ein wort
direkt auf das trommelfell geschrieben
die trommel fällt
lautlos
stimmhaft
ein wort
ein ort

一诗一书

一字
一谋杀案
当我开口
我不在那儿
一字
在其笼里
迷惑人也被迷惑
吐出报告
我那些往事
我那些卡片
没有言语
只有其影
我栖息其中
我影消失
无所估算
当我沉默
我乃相同原料所制
一如你
物质时间
在说一字

与啜饮一口水之间
那儿
乃肉体之音醒来之处
你不用耳朵也听见
一字
自其任务中解脱
一字
直接写进耳膜内
大鼓倒下
万籁俱寂
有声始出
一字
一地

A Poem for A Book

a word
a murder
when i speak
i am not there
a word
in its cage
arresting arrested
spits a report
about my crimes
about my cards
no word
only its shadow
in which i rest
my shadow disappears in it
nothing is judged
when i am silent
i am made of the same material
as you
material time
between one word

and a sip of water
there
where the voice awakes in the flesh
you hear without ears
a word
liberated from its duty
a word
written directly on the eardrum
the drum falls
soundless
voiced
a word
a place

(Translated by Emily Sullivan)

Ges-ICH-ter

*1

Seitdem ich auf dieser Welt geboren bin, habe ich niemals mein Gesicht von außen gesehen. Kein Spiegel zeigt mir, wie ich im Gespräch mit einer anderen Person aussehe. Oft sehe ich im Gesicht der anderen rätselhafte Züge. Sie faszinieren mich, und ich widerspiegele sie auf meinem Gesicht. Mein Gesicht ist ein Skizzenbuch. Die Person, die mit mir spricht, entdeckt in meinem Gesicht Zeichnungen der eigenen Gesichtszüge und steigt in sie ein, sowie man in einen Fernzug steigt.

*2

Ich weiß nicht, wie ich von außen aussehe. Von innen aber habe ich mein Gesicht schon oft gesehen: Eine schattige Landschaft mit einem sumpfigen Wald und zwei gefrorenen Seen. Außerdem gibt es dort eine Tropfsteinhöhle und zwei Tunnel mit Muscheln im Netz. Ich trete in diese Landschaft ein und verlaufe mich.

*3

Ich kann nicht das Gesicht jener Frau von innen sehen. So werde ich zu einem Wind und streichele die Oberfläche ihres Gesichtes. Ihr Gesicht ist eine menschenlose Landschaft. Der Wind liest die Blindenschrift, die auf dem Feld geschrieben ist. Langsam werden zwei Seen auf dem Feld sichtbar. Tasten ist Sehen ohne Distanz. Wenn es weht, rauschen blonde Gräser und graublaues Wasser.

*4

In der Tropfsteinhöhle, aus der der blinde Wind bläst, lebt ein nacktes Ungeheuer mit rötlicher, feuchter Haut. Der Boden ist klebrig naß und glänzt blutrot. Der Unterleib des Ungeheuers ist an dem Boden festgewachsen. Es knurrt nicht, heult nicht, spricht nicht. Wenn das Tier sich aber bewegt, entsteht ein stöhnender Wind. Er fliegt aus der Höhle heraus und verwandelt sich in Wörter.

*5

Ein blinder Wind entsteht in einer Landschaft und bewegt sich in eine andere. Dann kehrt er zurück oder zieht weiter in eine dritte Landschaft. Der Wind gehört keinem Ort.

Es wird auf einmal still, und dann weht es wieder.

Ist dieser Wind ein anderer als der letzte? Wie kann man Luftzüge auseinanderhalten? Hat ein Wind ein Gesicht?

*6

Ich sehe das Gesicht des Windes, wenn das Wasser Lachfalten zeigt oder Grimassen schneidet. Ich sehe sein Gesicht, wenn das letzte Blatt am Baum mit dem Kopf schüttelt. Das Gesicht des Windes ist das, was er in Bewegung setzt.

我脸有众

*1

自降生以来，我未尝从外探视我脸。未尝有镜子照现我，犹如我与他人对话。我常自他人的脸读出各种神秘，迷惑着我，而我脸复又展示它们。我脸是速写簿。那与我对话者，自我脸发现他自己的特征，并自此进入，如同踏上长途列车。

*2

我不知道从外看来我形象何如。从内观之，我倒看见我脸很多次了，一片幽暗之地上，有一个沼泽森林与两个冰冻湖泊。此外网中尚有一座钟乳洞及两条有贝类的隧道。我走进并迷失于如是景观中。

*3

从内里我看不见那女子的脸。所以我转为风轻抚她的脸庞。她脸是没人的山水。风阅读在田野写就的盲文。两座湖泊在野外缓缓浮现。摸索是没距离的观看。当风吹过，金色的草与灰蓝的水窃窃私语。

*4

钟乳洞内，风无定向，一头赤裸的怪物皮相鲜红湿润。潮湿地面暗红闪耀。怪物的腹部扎根大地。它不狂哮，不哭，不说话。但当怪物移动自己，萧萧风声形成。它飞出洞外自成言辞。

*5

盲目的风于景色中浮现，又移往他处。然后它又折回或是前往第三处景观。风并不属于任何地方。随即安静下来了，然后风再起。今天的风抄袭了昨天的么？谁又可区分这些气流？一种风亦有一种脸容吗？

*6

我看见风之脸，当水展露笑靥或扮鬼脸。我看见风之脸，当树上最后的叶子轻轻摇头。风的脸，如它动静。

v-I-sages

* 1

Ever since I was born into this world, I have never seen my face from the outside. Not a single mirror shows me how I look in a conversation with another person. Often I see puzzling traits in others' faces. They fascinate me, and on my face I reflect them. My face is a sketchbook. The person who is speaking with me discovers drawings of their own facial traits in my face and steps into them, as one steps into a train.

* 2

I don't know how I look from the outside. I have, however, seen my face from the inside often enough: a shadowy landscape with a swampy forest and two frozen lakes. Besides that there is a cave of stalactites and two tunnels with clams in nets. I enter this landscape and get lost.

* 3

I can't see that woman's face from the inside. So I turn into a wind and stroke the surface of her face. Her face is a humanless landscape. The wind reads the Braille that is written on her face. In that moment two lakes become visible in the field. Touching is seeing without distance. When it blows, blond grass and gray-blue water rustle.

* 4

In the stalactite cave, out of which the wind blows, lives a naked monster with reddish, moist skin. The floor is sticky wet and gleams blood red. The abdomen of the monster has grown stuck to the floor. It does not growl, does not howl, does not speak. However, when the animal moves, a moaning wind emerges. It flies out of the cave and transforms itself into words.

* 5

A blind wind emerges from a landscape and moves in another. Then it turns back or pulls further into a third landscape. The wind does not belong to any place. Suddenly it becomes quiet, and then it blows again. Is this wind different from the last? How can you differentiate between drafts? Does a wind have a face?

* 6

I see the face of the wind, when the water shows laughter wrinkles or makes faces. I see its face, when the last leaf on the tree shakes its head. The wind's face is what it puts into motion.

(Translated by Emily Sullivan)

Die Rosinenaugen

Dienstags esse ich gerne meinen Vater. Er schmeckt nach Hirsch. Er ist aus Brotteig gemacht. Ich weiß, daß er in Wirklichkeit eine Frau ist. Man darf ihn das aber nicht sagen, sonst werden seine Augen hohl. Wenn der Herd heiß wird und die Sonne untergeht, flüstert ihm sein toter Bruder ins Ohr: Du bist doch eine Frau. Aus Brotteig ist er gemacht. Seine Zitzen sind aus schwarzen Rosinen gemacht. Die Augen einer Frau, die er gestern im Gefängnis besuchte, waren auch aus Rosinen gemacht. Mein Vater hat schwarze Zitzen. Ich habe sie noch nie gesehen, denn sie sind ins Fleisch seiner Brust eingegraben. Wie Mutter und Tochter liegen sie nebeneinander und haben kaltes Fieber. Einmal am Tag wachen sie auf und springen aus seinem Fleisch wie ein Geschrei. Mein Vater erzählt mir von Ihnen, denn er weiß, daß sie mir gefallen werden. Aber er zeigt sie mir nicht und drückt sie zurück, bevor ich meine Augen öffne. Brot esse ich meistens kalt. Beim Kauen empfinde ich Wärme in seinem Fleisch. Ich kaue und kaue und bilde mir ein, daß ich weiter kaue. In Wirklichkeit kaue ich nicht mehr, sondern blicke und finde die Rosinen im Ofen. Sie sind angebrannt und riechen nach dem Schatten eines Hirsches. Eine Frau hatte in diesem Haus gelebt. Als mein Vater einzog, wurde sie entführt. An das Gesicht der Frau kann ich mich nicht mehr erinnern. Ich ärgere mich und esse weiter. Ich setze mich auf den Stuhl und esse weiter. Denn ich esse gern meinen Vater. Dabei erinnert er sich an die Frau und wiederholt ihre Worte, die er ihr beigebracht hat: Wer auf dem Stuhl sitze, müsse stehen wollen. Wer in der Küche stehe, müsse fliegen wollen. Fliegen könnte ich ohne Mühe, wenn ich nicht mehr essen würde. Aber ich esse weiter und werde immer schwerer. Ich wünsche mir, daß ich aus Rosinen gemacht bin. In der Sprache der Rosinen spreche ich: Nenne mich nicht bei einem Ortsnamen. Schenke mir keine Damenschuhe. Es ist die Nacht des Mädchenfestes. Mein Vater schenkt mir einen Damenlöffel. Ich kann nicht einschlafen, wenn mein

Bett nach angebranntem Hirsch riecht. Mein Vater sei früher ein Mann gewesen. Als er das Brot aus dem Ofen aß, wurde er zu einer Frau. Er hätte mir das aber nicht sagen dürfen. Ich wußte schon alles über ihn. Der Brotteig hatte mir das schon erzählt. Jetzt können wir nicht mehr unter einem Dach essen. Ich laufe weg von zuhause und habe nichts mehr zu verzehren. Am Ende der Stadt steht ein Haus. Die Tür steht offen. Aus dem Haus riecht es nach Hirsch. Ich gehe hinein und sehe ein Bett. Es hat drei Beine. In dem Bett liegt mein Vater, der hier nicht sein kann. Sein Bauch ist weich und warm. In seinem Bauch schläft meine Mutter. Ich müßte noch lange warten, bis sie geboren wird. Denn er will sie noch nicht gehen lassen. Sonst muß ich an seinem Bauch weiter essen, bis ich sie erreiche. Ich stehe im Garten und frage den Apfelbaum, was mit ihr passieren wird. Ich höre wie zwei Menschen zusammen atmen. Einer schläft im Bauch des Anderen. Der Bauch ist aus Brotteig gemacht. Ich habe keinen Hunger. Ich muß nicht Hunger haben, um das Brot essen zu wollen. Es ist dunkel und die Laterne wirft den Schatten eines Jägers. Wenn es mein Vater ist, werde ich ihn töten, bevor er die Schlafende erschießt. Es ist mein Vater. Ich habe kein Gewehr. Er schreit und fällt. Tief in seinem Bauch steckt eine Todeskugel als Beweis für den Mord. Ich habe nichts getan. Aus dem Bauch starren zwei Rosinenaugen. Zwei Menschen sind tot, und der dritte überlebt.

葡萄干眼睛

逢周二我喜欢吃父亲的肉，味如鹿身，却由面团制成。我知道，事实上他是女子。但人们不应向他提及，以免他的眼睛变得空洞。当烤箱是热的，而太阳下山时，他死去的兄弟向他窃窃私语：你终究是一名女子。他由面团制成，乳头则是黑葡萄干。他昨日到监狱探访的女子的眼睛，也一样是黑葡萄干。我父有黑色乳头。我还未见过，因它们深深隐进他胸膛里。它们像母女俩一样并排躺在冷汗里。每天一次，她们转醒并如一声尖叫般从他肉身中蹦跳出来。我父告诉我，他知道我会喜欢她们。但他并不向我展现她们，并在我睁眼之前就把她们推回体内。我总吃冷面包。咀嚼时，我就从其肉中吃出温暖。我咀嚼复咀嚼并想象我仍会一直咀嚼。事实上我并没继续下去，却在烤箱里看见及找到一些葡萄干。它们烧过，散发鹿的影子的气味。女子曾在这所房子里居住。我父迁入后，她被绑票。在女子的脸上我找不到记认的痕迹。我很生气并重新进食，我坐在椅子上一直吃食。因我喜欢吃我父。所以他记起那女子并复述她的言语，那是他早前教予她的：谁坐于椅子上，谁就想站起来；谁站在厨房里，谁就想起飞。当我不再进食，我就能轻易起飞。但我总在吃，一切变得困难。我希望我是由葡萄干制成的。在葡萄干的语言里我言说：不要命名我为一个地方，不要给我任何女性的鞋子，这是女孩晚上的盛宴。我父给了我女用汤匙。我无法入睡，当我的床缠绕着鹿肉烧焦的气味。我父曾是男子，当他吃着出炉面包，他变性为女身。他没有跟我提及过，但我知道关于他的一切，面团已告知我。现在我们不能在一个屋檐下吃饭，我离家出走，身上也没有任何吃的。一所房子在小镇尽头。门是敞开的。屋子里有鹿的气味。我走进去看见一张床，有三条腿，我父躺在床上，他不应在这儿。他的肚子轻软暖和，我母睡在里头。我仍得久久等待她的诞生，因为我父不让她离去。我得一直吃他的肚子，直至触到我母。我站在花园里向苹果树发问：将有何事降在汝身？我听到恍如两人在呼吸。其一睡在另一个的腹内，那面包制成的肚子。我不感到饿，不应再感到饿，也不应欲求面包。黑暗来临，灯笼蒙上猎人的阴影。若我父在，我则弑之，早在他拍摄那熟睡者之前。那是我父。我没有枪。他尖叫他跌倒。他肚子深处的死亡之球是谋杀的证据。我什么也没做过。肚子上两颗葡萄干眼睛瞅着我。两个人死去了，第三个存活下来。

Raisin Eyes

On Tuesdays I like to eat my father. He tastes of venison. Bread dough is what he's made of. I know he's really a woman. But you can't say this to his face or his eyes will turn hollow hollow out. When the fire is hot and the sun goes down, his dead brother whispers in his ear: you're a woman. He's made of bread dough. His nipples are raisins. The eyes of a woman he went to see in prison yesterday were also raisins. My father has black nipples. I've never seen them, they are buried deep in the flesh of his chest. Like mother and daughter they lie side by side in a cold sweat. Once a day they wake up and leap out of his flesh like a scream. My father tells me about them because he knows I'll like them. But he doesn't show them to me, he presses them back into place before I open my eyes. Usually I eat my bread cold. As I chew I feel the warmth of his flesh. I chew and chew and imagine I am continuing to chew. In reality I stop chewing and look around and find the raisins in the oven. They are burnt and smell like the shadow of a stag. A woman once lived in this house. When my father moved in, she was abducted. I can no longer recall the woman's face. I feel annoyed and go on eating. I sit down on the chair and go on eating. For I like eating my father. It makes him think of the woman and repeat her words, which he taught to her: Whoever sits on the chair must want to stand. Whoever stands in the kitchen must want to fly. I could fly without effort if I stopped eating. But I go on eating and grow heavier and heavier. I wish I were made of raisins. In the language of raisins I say: do not call me by a place name. Do not give me women's shoes. It is the night of the festival of girls. My father gives me a women's spoon. I can't sleep when my bed smells of burnt venison. My father tells me he used to be a man. When he ate bread from the oven, he became a woman. He shouldn't have told me that. I knew everything about him. The bread dough told me ages ago. Now we can no longer go on eating under one roof. I run away from home and have nothing left to eat. At the edge of town stands a house. The door is ajar. From the house comes the smell of venison. I go in and see a bed. It has three legs. In the bed lies my father, who can't possibly be here. His belly is soft and warm. In his belly, my mother sleeps. I'd have to wait a long time for her to be born. He doesn't want to let her go yet. Otherwise I'll have to keep eating away at his belly until I reach her. I stand in the garden and ask the apple tree what will become of her. I can hear two people breathing in unison. One sleeps in the other's belly. The belly is made of bread dough. I'm not hungry. I don't have to be hungry to want to eat the bread. It is dark now, and the lantern casts the shadow of a hunter. If it is my father, I will kill him before he can shoot the sleeping woman. It is my father. I have no gun. He gives a cry and falls. A fatal bullet is embedded in his belly as proof of the murder. I didn't do anything. From his belly, two raisin eyes peer out. Two people are dead, and the third survives.

(Translated by Susan Bernofsky)

作者简介

多和田叶子，用日、德双语写作的小说家和诗人，1960年生于东京。1982年移居德国，后来在苏黎世大学获得德国文学博士学位。1993年以短篇小说《倒插门的狗女婿》获芥川奖，她1996年获德国“沙米索文学奖”，2005年获德意志联邦共和国歌德勋章。被译成英文的小说包括《倒插门的狗女婿》（1998）、《欧陆开始的地方》（2002）、《面对桥梁》（2007）、《裸眼》（2009）等。

Yoko Tawada was born in Tokyo in 1960. She was educated at Waseda University and has lived in Germany since 1982. She received her Ph.D. in German literature from the University of Zurich. She writes in both German and Japanese and was awarded the prestigious Akutagawa Prize in 1993 for her short story *The Bridegroom Was a Dog*. In 1996, she won the Adelbert von Chamisso Prize. In 2005, she was awarded the Goethe Medal, an official decoration of the Federal Republic of Germany. English translations of her fiction include *The Bridegroom Was a Dog* (Kodansha International, 1998), *Where Europe Begins* (New Directions, 2002), *Facing the Bridge* (New Directions, 2007), and *The Naked Eye* (New Directions, 2009).

图书在版编目（CIP）数据

一诗一书：德汉英对照 /（日）多和田叶子著；田原，毛乙馨，方太初译.
-- 南京：江苏凤凰文艺出版社,2021.1

（红狐丛书. 一衣带水的相望）

ISBN 978-7-5594-1387-1

Ⅰ. ①一… Ⅱ. ①多… ②田… ③毛… ④方…
Ⅲ. ①诗集－日本－现代－德、汉、英 Ⅳ. ①I313.25

中国版本图书馆CIP数据核字(2017)第272934号

红狐丛书·一衣带水的相望：一诗一书

北岛 主编
（日）多和田叶子 著
毛乙馨 方太初 译

出 版 人 张在健
责任编辑 王娱瑶 于奎潮
特约编辑 薛 倩 傅春晖
书籍设计 周伟伟
责任印制 刘 巍
出版发行 江苏凤凰文艺出版社
南京市中央路165号，邮编：210009
出版社网址 http://www.jswenyi.com
印 刷 苏州越洋印刷有限公司
开 本 880×1230毫米 1/32
印 张 2.75
字 数 35千字
版 次 2021年1月第1版
印 次 2021年1月第1次印刷
标准书号 ISBN 978-7-5594-1387-1
定 价 128.00元（全七册）

红狐丛书·东亚卷 | 北岛 主编

Man Without Arms

没胳膊的男人

腕のない男

Hirata Toshiko

［日］平田俊子 著 田原 邓阳璐 译

江苏凤凰文艺出版社
JIANGSU PHOENIX LITERATURE AND ART PUBLISHING

目录

Contents

Man Without Arms

Hirata Toshiko

ひ・と・び・と

あなたの声を聞かせてください
わたしの声を聞いてください

あなたの好きな窓を描いてください
わたしの好きな色にぬらせてください

あなたの湖をちょっと貸してください
わたしの山にのぼってもいいよ

あなたの鎖骨を見せてください
わたしのと片っぽ交換しましょう

あなたの運命線を見せてください
わたしの生命線を少しあげます

あなたの物語にさわらせてください
わたしの歴史を抱きしめてください

あなたの傷を見せてください
わたしの傷あとも見てください

あなたの泣き顔を見せてください
わたしも泣くからそばにいてほしい

あなたが生まれた町の
地図を描いてください
いつかいっしょに行けたらいいね

あなたの影を見せてください
わたしの影と並べてみましょう
きっとふたつはとてもよく似ている

あなたの名前を教えてください
わたしの名前も尋ねてください

人们

请让我听听你的声音
请听听我的声音

请画下你喜欢的窗口
让我涂上我喜欢的颜色

请把你的湖泊借我一下
你也可以攀上我的山峦

请让我看看你的锁骨
跟我交换一根吧

请让我看看你手上的命运线
我会给你一截儿我的生命线

请让我触摸你的故事
抱紧我的历史

请让我看看你的伤口
也请你看看我的伤痕

请让我看看你的哭容
因为我也哭泣，想让你待在我身旁

请画出你出生的城市
什么时候能跟你一起去该有多好啊

请让我看看你的影子
若与我的影子并肩
它们一定很相似

请告诉我你的名字
也请你问问我的名字

P-E-O-P-L-E

Please let me hear your voice
Please listen to my voice

Please draw a window you like
Please let me paint the color I like

Please lend me your lake
Feel free to climb my mountain

Please show me your collarbone
Let's exchange one of yours for mine

Please show me your line of fortune
I'll give you part of my life line

Please let me touch your narrative
Please embrace my history

Please show me your wounds
Please take a look at my scars

Please show me what you look like in tears
I also cry so I'd like you by my side

Please draw me a map
Of the town where you were born
Once day I'd like to go there with you

Please show me your shadow
Let's line yours up with mine
No doubt the two will look a lot alike

Please tell me your name
Please ask me my name as well

(Translated by Jeffrey Angles)

腕のない男

腕のない男が立っていた
吊り橋のような横断歩道をはさんで
わたしと男はむきあっていた
男の腕は二本ともなかった
信号が青になり男はやってくる
心配事があるふりをして
靴を見ながらわたしは歩いた
男とすれ違い
むこう岸について
橋を落としたあとでふりむき
男の古い上着を見た
上着の二本のからっぽの袖が
風になびくのをしばらく眺めた

腕はわたしが切ったのだ
余分な枝をはらうみたいに
鋸でギリリと切断した
ハンドルを握れないように
キーボードをたたけないように
ドアを開けて出ていかないように
女のところにいかないように

女の乳房をつかめないよう
女の首をしめられないよう
力いっぱい鋸を引いた
初めてにしては上手にできた
男も「うまい」とほめてくれた
腕を落とした男のからだは
冬の木のように簡潔になった
でも

腕は何度でもはえてくる
女の部屋にたどりつくころには
上着の二本のからっぽの袖は
枝のようなものでふくらんでいるのだ
胴体をまっぷたつに切ったところで
腕は何度でもはえてくるのだ

没胳膊的男人

没胳膊的男人站着
隔着像吊桥似的人行横道
与我面对面
男人的两条胳膊都没了
绿灯亮后，他走过来
我装作满腹心事
一边看着鞋子迈步
与他擦身而过
来到彼岸
在拆掉桥的痕迹上我转过脸
对着穿旧上衣的男人
那两只空荡荡随风飘动的
袖子眺望了很久

胳膊是我砍掉的
像除去多余的枝条
嚓嚓嚓地用锯拉断
为了让他握不住方向盘
为了让他无法敲按键盘
为了不让他开门外出
去找女人

为了让他抓不住女人的乳房
和无法掐住女人的脖颈
我用尽全力拉动锯子
虽为新手，我却锯得得心应手
男人也满口称赞我“老练”
掉了两条胳膊的男人之躯
像冬天的树木一样简单
不过

胳膊会无数次地长出来
在他好容易才走到女人的房间时
上衣上那空荡荡的两只袖子
鼓起了像枝条一样的东西
即使把他的躯体锯成两截儿
胳膊还会无数次地长出来

Man Without Arms

A man was standing there without arms
He and I faced each other across the crosswalk
Suspended between us like a rope bridge
The man didn't have either of his arms
He walked this way when the light turned green
I looked at my shoes as I walked
Pretending to be worried
I walked by him
Once I had reached the other side
Once I had cut the bridge down, I turned to look
I looked at the man's old jacket
I watched as the two empty sleeves
Of his jacket fluttered in the wind

I was the one who cut off his arms
I amputated them with a saw
Like getting rid of two extra branches
So he couldn't hold the steering wheel
So he couldn't play the keyboard
So he couldn't open the door and go
So he couldn't go where she was

So he couldn't grab her breast
So he couldn't strangle her
I sawed with all my might
I did it well, considering it was my first time
Even he complimented me on my skill
The body of the armless man
Was as clean as a tree in winter
But

Arms grow back over and over again
When he reaches her room
The two empty sleeves of his jacket
Will have filled out like branches
Even when I split him clean in two
The arms grow back over and over again

(Translated by Jeffrey Angles)

カメラ

わたしのかわいい寝顔をあなたは撮る
わたしの無邪気な笑顔をあなたは撮る
わたしの大きな胸をあなたは撮る
撮らないでくれといったのに

わたしの肩のほくろをあなたは撮る
わたしの脱いだブラウスをあなたは撮る
わたしの汚れた部屋をあなたは撮る
撮らないでくれといったのに

わたしが怒鳴られるところをあなたは撮る
わたしが殴られるところをあなたは撮る
わたしが蹴飛ばされるところをあなたは撮る
撮られたことをわたしは知らない

わたしの家が燃えるところをあなたは撮る
わたしの弟が落ちるところをあなたは撮る
わたしの妹が倒れるところをあなたは撮る
わたしの兄が爆死するところをあなたは撮る
わたしの姉が自決するところをあなたは撮る
わたしの母が泣くところをあなたは撮る

撮るなといわなかったから？

わたしのかさかさの手足をあなたは撮る
わたしのむくんだ顔をあなたは撮る
わたしのゆがんだ背骨をあなたは撮る
わたしの抜け落ちた髪をあなたは撮る
撮るなという力は残っていない

これはだめ　これはよし
これはだめ　これはよし
モニターを見ながら
あなたは
写真を選ぶ
生き残るわたし
消されるわたし
（生き残るわたし
（消されるわたし
消したからといって
撮らなかったことにはならない
（消したからといって
（撮らなかったことにはならない

あなたは撮り
そして消しました
(あなたは撮り
(そして消しました
たくさんのわたしが撮られました
たくさんのわたしが消されました
撮られた数よりたくさんのわたしが
指一本で消えました

照相机

你拍我可爱的睡颜
你拍我纯真的笑脸
你拍我的大胸
虽然说过不要拍了

你拍我肩上的黑痣
你拍我脱下的衬衣
你拍我脏乱的房间
虽然说过不要拍了

你拍我被吼的样子
你拍我被打的样子
你拍我被踢飞的样子
我不知道你拍了

你拍我家着火的样子
你拍我弟弟坠落的样子
你拍我妹妹倒下的样子
你拍我哥哥被炸死的样子
你拍我姐姐自杀的样子
你拍我母亲哭泣的样子

因为没告诉你不要拍吗

你拍我粗糙的手
你拍我浮肿的脸
你拍我弯曲的背
你拍我掉落的头发
我已经无力说不要拍了

这张不行　这张可以
这张不行　这张可以
你一边看屏幕
一边挑选照片
幸存的我
被消去的我
（幸存的我
（被消去的我
虽说已经消去了
但不能说没拍过
（虽说已经消去了
（但不能说没拍过
你拍了

然后消去
（你拍了
（然后消去
许多的我被拍过
许多的我被消去
许多被拍的我
完美地消失了

Camera

You take my sweet sleeping face
You take my innocent smile
You take my large breasts
Even though I asked you not to

You take the mole on my shoulder
You take the blouse I have taken off
You take my dirty room
Even though I asked you not to

You take me when I am angry
You take me when I get hit
You take me when I get kicked across the room
Even though I do not know you have done it

You take my house when it is burning
You take my younger brother when he is falling
You take my younger sister when she is collapsing
You take my older brother when he burns to death
You take my older sister when she kills herself
You take my mother as she is weeping

Is that because I didn't tell you not to take them?

You take the dry skin on my arms and legs
You take my swollen face
You take my crooked spine
You take my hair that has fallen out
I no longer have the strength to tell you no

This one's no good, this one's good
This one's no good, this one's good
As you look at the monitor
You choose the photos
The versions of me that survive
The versions of me that are erased
(The versions of me that survive
(The versions of me that are erased
Even if you erase me
It does not mean you didn't take me
(Even if you erase me
(It does not mean you didn't take me
You took me

And erased me
(You took me
(And erased me
You took lots of me
You erased lots of me
More of me than what you took
Disappeared with the work of a single finger

(Translated by Jeffrey Angles)

寒い春

豆を挽いて
お湯を少しずつそそぎ
コーヒーを二杯淹れる
一杯は自分のため
もう一杯は　ここにいない人のため

寒がりだったから
マフラーを巻いてあげればよかった
手袋を持たせてあげればよかった
何もないままいかせてしまった
悔恨の炎で沸かすのは
冷たすぎる水

生は苦しく　死は優しい
そんなふうに思えば救われるだろうか
風の甘さや光のまぶしさに
気づかないふりをして

花が咲いて　鳥がさえずり
誰かがいない春
感情のかけらがひとりごとになって
いくらでもこぼれ落ちる

お湯はいつでも沸かしておこうよ
寒い人を暖められるよう
すぐにコーヒーを淹れられるよう
誰も帰ってこない日も

寒春

我磨碎了豆子
慢慢注入热水
冲两杯咖啡
一杯为自己
另一杯　为不在这里的人

因为你怕冷
给你围上围巾就好了
给你戴上手套就好了
就那样什么也没做就让你走了
用悔恨的火焰烧开了
那冷得过分的水

活着痛苦　死了轻松
如果这样想　就能得到救赎吗
假装不在意
风的清甜与日光的耀眼

花开　鸟鸣
他不在的春天
感情的碎片化为自言自语
碎落一地

无论什么时候让热水总开着吧
为了能温暖冰冷的人
为了能马上冲出一杯咖啡
即使是在没人回来的日子

Cold Spring

I grind the beans
Pour in the hot water little by little
And make two cups of coffee
One for me
The other for someone no longer here

You were susceptible to cold
I should have wrapped a scarf around you
I should have given you gloves
But I sent you off empty-handed
The too-cold water boils
With flames of regret

Life is hard, death is easy
Does it help to think that way?
In the bright light and sweet wind
I pretend not to know the answer

Flowers bloom, birds sing
Spring comes without a certain someone
Fragments of feeling muttered to myself
Spill over, more than I can count

I will keep the water always at a boil
So that those who are cold may warm themselves
So that I can make coffee at a moment's notice
Even on the days no one will return

(Translated by Jeffrey Angles)

Translator's Note:
Hirata published this poem in March 2015 to commemorate the fourth anniversary of the 2011 disasters and the seventieth anniversary of the end of World War II.

ゆれるな

ゆれるね
きょうもゆれてるね
地球が荒ぶるゆりかごだったとは
知らなかったよ
おとなも子どもも眠らせない
意地悪なゆりかごだったとは

三月なんだよ春なんだよ
春眠あかつきを覚えない
優しい季節のはずなのに
今年の春は
ひとをゆさぶり
眠らせまいとする

地球よ　お前は
いつの日も
愉快にまわるだけでいい
ゆれるのは
風に吹かれる花や
庭の洗濯物にまかせて
お前はいつも
無邪気にまわれ

地球をゆらすものは
泡となって消えろ
ゆれるな
れるな
るな
な
な
な！

别摇晃啦

摇晃了吧
今天也摇晃了吧
以前不知道
地球是暴乱的摇篮
大人和孩子都无法安睡
是故意使坏的摇篮

是三月啊　是春天啊
却不知是春眠之际
本来应该是温柔的季节
但今年的春天
摇晃着
让人无法安睡

地球啊　你啊
无论什么时候
开心就好了
摇晃的事
就交给风吹过的花儿
院子里晾的衣服吧
你只要
天真地旋转

摇晃地球的东西
化成泡沫消失吧
别摇啦
别摇
别
别
别!

Do Not Tremble

It trembles
It is trembling again today
I did not know that the earth
Is an unruly cradle
A cruel cradle that lets
Neither adult nor child sleep

It is March, it is spring
It should be a gentle season of vernal sleep
When one sleeps so deeply there is no dawn
But spring this year
Shakes us to keep us
From falling asleep

Earth, it is enough
For you simply to
Keep spinning happily
Leave the trembling
To windblown flowers and
Laundry hanging in the year
You should simply spin
Innocently

Those forces that shake the earth

May you turn to bubbles and disappear

Do not tremble

Do not trem

Do not tre

Do not

Not

No!

(Translated by Jeffrey Angles)

宝物

世界で一番美しい言葉はコンセルトヘボウです

四年前のアムステルダム
午後のトラムにゆられていると
大きな建て物が前方に見えた
あれは何？　と尋ねると
コンセルトヘボウとあなたは答えた

コンセルトヘボウ
そのときの私には
それが何だかわからなかった
ただ　こうつぶやいたときの
あなたの声がとてもきれいで
以来この言葉は私の宝物になった

誰かがこの言葉を口にするのを
それまでも
そのあとも聞いたことはない
あなたがこの言葉をつぶやいたのも
あのときだけだ
ただ一度だけ耳にした言葉

私だけが聞いた
あのときの
あなたの
柔らかな
声

ここにこうして書いてしまうと
宝物はたちまち輝きを失い
蝉の死骸以下のものになる
大切なものを捨て去るために
私は秘密を打ち明けた
この言葉もあなたのことも
忘れるために

さよなら
私のコンセルトヘボウ
ときめくことはもうないでしょう
大切なものは何度でも
捨てなければなりません

別離がもたらすはずの甘い露さえ
ここに書くことで薄まってしまった
私は少しも傷ついていない
そのことを残念に思う

宝物

世上最优美的词语是皇家音乐厅管弦乐团

四年前的阿姆斯特丹
坐在下午的电车里摇摇晃晃
看见前方巨大的建筑物
那是什么？我问
你回答那是皇家音乐厅管弦乐团

皇家音乐厅管弦乐团
此时的我
并不知道那是什么
只是　你轻言轻语的时候
声音很美
之后这词语就成了我的宝物

这之前
这之后　都再也没听过
谁再把这个词语挂在嘴边
你悄声对我说这个词语
也只有那个时候
仅此一次的耳语

只有我听见
那时
你
温柔的
声音

这样写下来
宝物忽然就失去了它的光彩
连蝉的尸骸都不如
为了舍去这珍贵的东西
我说出了秘密
为了忘却
这词语和你

再见
我的皇家音乐厅管弦乐团
怦然心动的东西已经消失了吧
宝贵的东西必须要扔
很多次

甚至连本该别离带来的甘露
也因此在这里变得淡了
我没有受伤
只觉遗憾

Treasure

The most beautiful word in the world is Concertgebouw

Four years ago in Amsterdam
Shaken by the afternoon train
I spied a large building before us
What's that? I asked
The Concertgebouw, you answered

Concertgebouw
At the time I didn't know
What that meant
But when you whispered the word
Your voice was so lovely
That I have treasured it ever since

Until then I had never heard
Anyone utter that word
Nor have I since
The only time you whispered it
Was on that day
A word heard only once

That I alone heard
Your
Soft
Voice
That day

Writing it down like this
My treasure quickly loses its luster
Becoming less than a discarded cicada husk
I revealed this secret
To get rid of something dear
To forget both
You and that word

Goodbye
My Concertgebouw
My heart will never again beat quickly for you
One has to dispose of what is precious
Over and over again

Even the sweet dew of separation
Grows thin as I write about it here
I am not the least bit hurt
And that, I think, is
The most unfortunate part

(Translated by Jeffrey Angles)

私見、ゴッホの「寝室」

この部屋には二つの椅子がある
どちらも素朴な木の椅子だ
性別は　不明
年齢も　不明
二つの素材は不明だが
左の椅子は
右の椅子より大人びている
左が兄で　右が妹なのだろう

椅子と椅子の間にはテーブルがある
テーブルはやつれた顔をしている
椅子とテーブルの間に
恋愛関係はない
あるのは親子関係で
テーブルは椅子たちの母である

この部屋で一番目立つのはベッド
部屋の面積のほぼ半分を占めている
二つの椅子とテーブルをあわせたよりも
ベッドの体積ははるかに大きい
自分が巨漢であることを
ベッドは特に恥じてはいない

椅子とテーブルは立っているのに
ベッドは横たわっている
からだの具合が悪いのだ
「しっかりして　お父さん」
「しっかりして　あなた」
心配そうにベッドを見守る
妻と　二人の子供たち

夫はもう長くはないだろう
夫のからだを抜け出した血が
床を不吉な色に染めている
妻は水差しとコップを抱え
死に水を取る準備をしている

壁にかかった大きな布は
父の亡骸を覆うためのもの
それをするのは自分だと
兄はひそかに決めている

小さな妹は何もわからず
黙って父に寄り添っている

この絵を描いた画家は
後年　麦畑で自分を撃った
この絵を描いた画家は
生涯　家族に恵まれなかった

この部屋のベッドは
麦畑によく似た色をしている
この部屋の壁は
麦畑の上に広がる
空によく似た色をしている

观梵高的《寝室》有感

这个房间有两把椅子
都是朴素的木椅
性别不明
年龄不详
两把椅子的木材也无从知晓
左边的椅子
比右边的椅子更像大人
左边是哥哥，右边是妹妹吧

椅子与椅子之间摆着桌子
桌子显得愁容憔悴
椅子与桌子之间
不是恋爱关系
而是亲子关系
桌子是椅子的母亲

床在这个房间最醒目
占据着房间一半的空间
两把椅子和桌子合在一起
也没有床的体积大
床没有为自己是大汉
感到羞耻

椅子和桌子站立着
躺着的床
是身体出了毛病
“挺住啊，爸爸”
“坚强点啊，亲爱的”
妻子和两个孩子
仿佛担心地照看着床

丈夫将不久于人世
从丈夫身体抽出的血
把地板染成不吉的颜色
妻子抱着水壶和杯子
准备着润湿临终者嘴唇的“死水”

墙上挂着一大块布
是为了遮盖父亲的尸骨
这件事理应自己做
哥哥暗暗决定

年幼的妹妹什么都不知道
默默地靠着父亲

画这幅画的画家
几年后在麦田开枪自杀
画这幅画的画家
一生没有受惠于家庭

这个房间的床
跟麦田的颜色很像
这个房间的墙
在麦田之上扩展
跟天空的颜色很像

Van Gogh's Bedroom as I See It

There are two chairs in this room
Both are simple, unsophisticated chairs
Their gender is unclear
Their age also unclear
Both of them are simple but
The chair on the left is a little more grown up
Than the one on the right
Maybe it is the older brother
And the one on the left the younger sister

There is a table between the chairs
The table wears a worn out expression
The chairs and table are not lovers
Their relationship is that of parent and child
The table is mother to the chairs

What stands out most is the bed
Which takes up nearly half the room
The bed's volume is greater than that
Of the table and both chairs put together
Still, the bed is not especially ashamed
About what a giant it is

The chair and table are standing
But the bed is lying down
It is not doing so well these days
"Get better, daddy"
"Get better, darling"
The wife and her two children
Watch over it with worried expressions

The husband doesn't have much longer
The blood that has drained from him
Has stained the floor an ominous color
The wife holds a pitcher and cup
Ready to carry water to her dying husband

The large piece of cloth hanging on the wall
Is to shroud the father's corpse when he dies
The older brother has already secretly decided
That will be his job when the time comes

Unaware of what is happening
His little sister crowds close to her father
But does not utter a word

The artist who painted this
Shot himself in a wheat field at the end of his life
The artist who painted this
Was not blessed with family while he was alive

The color of the bed in the room
So strongly resembles the color of wheat
While the walls of the room
So strongly resemble the color of the sky
Stretching over the field of wheat

(Translated by Jeffrey Angles)

作者简介

平田俊子，日本当代著名诗人、作家。生于岛根县，毕业于立命馆大学文学部。1983年获得第一届《现代诗手帖》“现代诗新人奖”后，引起诗坛关注。1984年出版第一部诗集《报恩的薤》以来，相继出版有《大西洋极乐世界里的水盐味淡！》《夜夜发胖的女人》《快活夫妇》《信转雨》《现代诗文库·平田俊子诗集》等诗集。其诗集《终点站》获得“晚翠诗歌奖”，《诗歌一星期》获得“萩原朔太郎诗歌奖”。另外，还出版有多部小说集，其中《两人乘坐》获“野间文艺新人奖”，另有散文集《昨日的露珠》和戏剧集《走运的收音机》等。2016年最新诗集《戏言的自由》获得第26届紫式部文学奖。2003年与诗人谷川俊太郎、作家高桥源一郎三人合出的《活在日语中》一书中，以每人创作一篇小说、一首诗和写一个剧本之创意，给日本文坛带来了不少新的刺激。她的诗歌作品“在让故事性与诗歌的形式相抗衡的同时，以卓越的幽默感把潜伏在日常生活中的恐怖表面化”。1999年在NHK电视台举办的全国规模“诗歌拳击”比赛中，以语言和即兴诗作击败诗人白石嘉寿子而成为日本媒体一时关注的话题。

Hirata Toshiko (Japan) is a poet and novelist. During the 1980s, she, along with Hiromi Itō, emerged as one of the foremost voices so-called "women's boom" of poetry. Her poetry is known for its directness and black humor. Tāminaru (*Terminal*), the 1997 anthology from which most of the poems translated here came, won the Doi Bansui Prize for poetry. She has also won the Hagiwara Sakutarō Prize for poetry for her 2004 collection Shi *nanoka* (Poetry on the Seventh Day / Is This Poetry?). In recent years, she has increasingly turned to writing novels, which often feature ordinary people in bizarre circumstances that lead them to question the traditional family system and the spots allotted to them in society. Among her many novels are Piano sando (*Piano Sandwich,* 2001), Futari nori (*Two on Board,* 2004), which won the Noma Literary Prize for New Writers, and *Watashi no akakute yawarakana bubun* (*My Soft, Red Place,* 2007).

图书在版编目(CIP)数据

没胳膊的男人：日汉英对照 / (日) 平田俊子著；田原，邓阳璐译.
-- 南京：江苏凤凰文艺出版社，2021.1

(红狐丛书. 一衣带水的相望)

ISBN 978-7-5594-1387-1

Ⅰ.①没… Ⅱ.①平… ②田… ③邓… Ⅲ.①诗集-
日本-现代-日、汉、英 Ⅳ.①I313.25

中国版本图书馆CIP数据核字(2017)第272940号

红狐丛书·一衣带水的相望：没胳膊的男人

北岛 主编
(日)平田俊子 著
田原 邓阳璐 译

出 版 人 张在健
责任编辑 王娱瑶 于奎潮
特约编辑 薛 倩 傅春晖
书籍设计 周伟伟
责任印制 刘 巍
出版发行 江苏凤凰文艺出版社
南京市中央路165号，邮编：210009
出版社网址 http://www.jswenyi.com
印 刷 苏州越洋印刷有限公司
开 本 880×1230毫米 1/32
印 张 2.375
字 数 26千字
版 次 2021年1月第1版
印 次 2021年1月第1次印刷
标准书号 ISBN 978-7-5594-1387-1
定 价 128.00元(全七册)

江苏凤凰文艺版图书凡印刷、装订错误，可向出版社调换，联系电话025-83280257

红狐
RED FOX

活字文化
Moveable Type

ISBN 978-7-5594-1387-1
9 787559 413871 >
定价：128.00元
（全七册）

红狐丛书·东亚卷 | 北岛 主编

在机场写信

A Letter from the Airport

Moon Chung-Hee

［韩］文贞姬 著 薛舟 译

江苏凤凰文艺出版社
JIANGSU PHOENIX LITERATURE AND ART PUBLISHING

红狐丛书·东亚卷 | 北岛 主编

A Letter from the Airport

공항에서 쓸 편지

在机场写信

Moon Chung-Hee

［韩］文贞姬 著 薛舟 译

江苏凤凰文艺出版社
JIANGSU PHOENIX LITERATURE AND ART PUBLISHING

目录

Contents

A Letter from the Airport

Moon Chung-Hee

화장을 하며

입술을 자주색으로 칠하고 나니
거울 속에 속국의 공주가 앉아 있다
내 작은 얼굴은 국제 자본의 각축장
거상들이 만든 허구의 드라마가
명실공히 그 절정을 이룬다
좁은 영토에 만국기 펄럭인다

금년 가을 유행색은 섹시브라운
샤넬이 지시하는 대로 볼연지를 칠하고
예쁜 여자의 신화 속에
스스로를 가두니
이만하면 음모는 제법 완성된 셈
가끔 소스라치며
자신 속의 노예를 깨우치지만
매혹의 인공향과 부드러운 색조가 만든
착시는 이미 저항을 잃은 지 오래다

시간을 손으로 막기 위해 육체란
이렇듯 슬픈 향을 찍어 발라야 하는 것일까
안간힘처럼 에스테 로더의 아이라이너로
검은 철책을 두르고

디오르 한 방울을 귀밑에 살짝 뿌려 마무리한 후
드디어 외출 준비를 마친 속국의 여자는
비극 배우처럼 서서히 몸을 일으킨다

化妆

把嘴唇涂成紫色
附属国的公主坐在镜子里
我小小的脸蛋是国际资本的角逐场
巨商打造的虚构的电视剧
名副其实地达到了高潮
狭窄的领土上飘扬着万国旗

今年秋天流行性感的棕色
按照香奈尔的指示先擦胭脂
自我囚禁于
美丽女人的神话里
如果到此为止，阴谋已算完成
偶尔毛骨悚然
意识到内心的奴隶
魅惑的人工香和柔和的色调
制造出错觉，错觉早已失去了抵抗

为了用手阻挡时间
肉体需要涂抹如此悲伤的香脂吗
竭尽全力用雅诗兰黛的眼线膏
围上黑色的栅栏

在鬓角下轻轻喷一滴迪奥
终于做好外出准备的附属国女人
像悲剧演员一样缓缓起身

Putting on Makeup

Painting my lips scarlet,
I see in the mirror a vain princess, all made up—
my small face an array of international cities,
a theater where fictitious dramas
staged by cosmetic illusions converge,
a miniature territory where the flags of all nations lavishly flutter.

Sexy brown is the color *à la mode* this fall.
Putting rouge on my cheeks, as Chanel instructs,
adhering to the myth of a glamorous woman,
I see the conspiracy is almost complete.
Occasionally frightened by the slavery in my mind—
yet once again bewitched by the artificial perfume
that enchants, by the hallucination drawn in softlytoned colors—

my protest is only feeble and sporadic.
To stop the winged chariots of time
With Estee Lauder eyeliner, I carefully
Draw a dark border around my eyes

And dab a drop of Christian Dior behind my ears,
The colonized Femme elegante ready to sortie!
She makes her entrance slowly, like a tragic heroine.

(Translated by Seong Kon Kim and Alec Gordon)

군인을 위한 노래

당신들은 모르실 거예요
이 땅에 태어난 여자들은
누구나 한때 군인을 애인으로 갖는답니다.
이 땅의 젊은 남자들은
누구나 군사 분계선으로 가서
목숨을 거기 내놓고 한 시절
형제라고 부르는 적을 향해 총을 겨누고
절박하게 고통과 그리움을 배운답니다.
그래서 이 땅의 여자들은
소녀 때는 위문편지를 쓰고
처녀 때는 군대로 면회를 간답니다.
그 시차 속에 가끔 사랑이 엇갈리는 일도 있어
어느 중년의 오후, 다시 돌아설 수 없는 길목에서
군복 벗은 그를 우연히 만나
서로 어쩔 줄 몰라 하며
속으로 조금 울기도 한답니다.
서로의 생 속에 군사 분계선보다 더 녹슨
어떤 선을 발견하고 슬퍼한답니다
당신들은 모르실 거예요
이 땅의 여자들은
누구나 한때 군인을 애인으로 갖는답니다

献给军人的歌

你们不会知道
出生于这片土地的女人
每个人都曾有过军人男友
这片土地上的年轻男人
每个人都曾去过军事分界线
临时交出自己的生命
枪口瞄准曾经称作兄弟的敌人
刻骨地学会痛苦和思念
这片土地上的女人
少女时代给军人写慰问信
少女时代去部队见面
爱情偶尔在这个时差里偏移
某个中年的下午
在无法转身的路口
和脱下军装的他偶遇
两个人不知所措
解释说也曾在心里轻轻啜泣
生命里发现了比军事分界线
锈得更严重的线，两个人为此伤感
你们不会知道
这片土地上的女人们
每个人都曾有过军人男友

Song for Soldiers

Perhaps you don't know this
but every woman in this land
once fell in love with a soldier.
All this land's young men
once went in uniform to the DMZ,
bearing arms against their brothers in the North
learning life's intense yearning and bittersweet agony.
Every woman in this land
wrote consoling letters to soldiers when young,
went to visit them at army camp when they grew up.
But love does not always ripen.
Often, in the passing years, paths diverged.
When, years later, a woman encounters
her old flame—dressed in a business suit
and in the sunset of his life—shy and embarrassed,
she silently cries at the realization
that a barrier rustier than the DMZ blocks the path of life.
Perhaps you don't know this,
but every woman in this land
once fell in love with a soldier.

(Translated by Seong Kon Kim, and Alec Gordon)

공항에서 쓸 편지

여보 일 년만 나를 찾지 말아 주세요
나 지금 결혼 안식년 휴가 떠나요
그날 우리 둘이 나란히 서서
기쁠 때나 슬플 때나 함께하겠다고
혼인 서약을 한 후
여기까지 용케 잘 왔어요
사막에 오아시스가 있고
아니 오아시스가 사막을 가졌던가요
아무튼 우리는 그 안에다 잔뿌리를 내리고
가지들도 제법 무성히 키웠어요
하지만, 일년만 나를 찾지 말아 주세요
병사에게도 휴가가 있고
노동자에게도 휴식이 있잖아요
조용한 학자들조차도
재충전을 위해 안식년을 떠나듯이
이제 내가 나에게 안식년을 줍니다
여보, 일 년만 나를 찾지 말아 주세요
내가 나를 찾아가지고 올 테니까요

在机场写信

亲爱的，一年之内不要找我
我要去度假，婚姻安息年
那天我们俩并肩而立
无论喜悦悲伤都会不离不弃
宣誓结婚之后
一路走到今天
沙漠有绿洲
不，应该说是绿洲拥有沙漠
我们在里面扎下须根
长出茂盛的枝叶
不过，一年之内不要找我
士兵都有假期
工人也会休假
甚至安静的学者
也有为自己充电的安息年
现在我要给自己一个安息年
亲爱的，一年之内不要找我
我会把自己找回来

A Letter from the Airport

Please, leave me alone for one year, my dear, my dear.
I'm on sabbatical from our marriage.
We've come a long way since our wedding vows
to stay together for better or for worse
until death do us part.
We settled at a desert oasis,
Rooted deeply and grew branches.
But please, for one year, don't try to follow me.
Soldiers needs to take leave.
A worker needs a holiday.
As quiet scholars go on sabbatical for replenishment,
I now take my well-earned leave.
So please don't look for me for a year, my dear.
I'll return when I've found myself.

(Translated by Seong Kon Kim and Alec Gordon)

남편

아버지도 아니고 오빠도 아닌
아버지와 오빠 사이의 촌수쯤 되는 남자
내게 잠 못 이루는 연애가 생기면
제일 먼저 의논하고 물어보고 싶다가도
아차, 다 되어도 이것만은 안 되지 하고
돌아누워 버리는
세상에서 제일 가깝고 제일 먼 남자
이 무슨 원수인가 싶을 때도 있지만
지구를 다 돌아다녀도
내가 낳은 새끼들을 제일로 사랑하는 남자는
이 남자일 것 같아
다시금 오늘도 저녁을 짓는다
그러고 보니 밥을 나와 함께
가장 많이 밥을 먹은 남자
전쟁을 가장 많이 가르쳐준 남자

丈夫

既不是父亲，也不是哥哥
关系介于父亲和哥哥之间
遇到辗转难眠的恋情
我首先想找他商量和咨询
天啊，别的都行，唯独这事不行
想到这里我又翻身躺下
世界上离我最近又最远的男人
有时感觉像是冤家对头
可是寻遍地球
最爱我生的孩子们的男人
恐怕还是他
今天我又做好了晚饭
突然想到，他是和我一起吃饭
次数最多的男人
关于战争，教我最多的男人

Husband

Neither father, nor brother,
but somewhere between. The two,
when a restless love keeps me awake,
I yearn to talk to him, alas
I can bare everything to him
But this; I spin
In bed
The closest, the farthest man on Earth
I'm amazed at times what a foe he is,
Yet he could be the one
who loves my babies best.
I cook dinner for him.
He, I realize, is the one I shared
most meals with, who taught me
how to fight.

(Translated by Clare You and Richard Silberg)

성공 시대

어떻게 하지? 나 그만 부자가 되고 말았네
대형 냉장고에 가득한 음식
옷장에 걸린 수십벌의 상표들
사방에 행복은 흔하기도 하지
언제든 부르면 달려오는 자장면
한 발만 살짝 얹으면 굴러가는 자동차
핸들을 이리저리 돌리기만 하면
나 어디든 갈수 있네
나 성공하고 말았네
이 시만 폐업하면 불행 끝
시 대신 진주 목걸이 하나만 사서 걸면 오케이
내 가슴에 피었다 지는 노을과 신록
아침 햇살보다 맑은 눈물
도둑고양이처럼 기어오르던 고독 다 귀찮아
시 파산 선고하고
행복 벤처 시작할까
그리고 저 캄캄한 도시 속으로
폭탄같이 강열한 차 하나 몰고
미친 듯이 질주 하기만 하면

成功时代

怎么办呢？我成了富翁
超大冰箱里满满的食物
挂在衣柜里的几十套名牌服装
幸福随处可见
随时能点的炸酱面外卖
轻轻放上右脚就能行驶的汽车
转转方向盘
我可以去任何地方
我成功了
现在停止写诗，不幸立刻结束
放弃诗歌，买条珍珠项链戴上就 OK
我心里绽放又凋零的晚霞和新绿
比晨光更清澈的眼泪
野猫般爬上来的孤独，我受够了
我要宣布诗歌破产
开始投资幸福
然后驾驶炸弹般猛烈的汽车
疯狂地冲进
漆黑的城市

The Age of Success

What shall I do? I've become rich!
Plenty of food in the fridge,
tons of brand new dresses in the closet—
happiness is everywhere!
Chinese food delivered instantly via phone.
a comfy car carrying me here and there—
if I take the wheel, I can go anywhere.
At last, I'm successful!
When I abandon poetry, all misery will fade away.
When I buy a pearl necklace, everything will be okay.
No more twilights and green pastures in my heart.
No more tears more clear than morning dew.
No more solitude, secretly, like an alley cat, creeping in
to announce the bankruptcy of poetry.
Shall I start the business of happiness?
Shall I madly dart, driving a powerful car
fast as speeding bullet, into the dark city?

(Translated by Seong Kon Kim and Alec Gordon)

남자를 위하여

남자들은
딸을 낳아 아버지가 될 때
비로소 자신 속에서 으르렁거리던 짐승과
결별한다
딸의 아랫도리를 바라보며
신이 나오는 길을 알게 된다
아기가 나오는 곳이
바로 신이 나오는 곳임을 깨닫고
문득 부끄러워 얼굴 붉힌다
딸에게 뽀뽀를 하며
자신의 수염이 때로 독가시였음도 안다
남자들은
딸을 낳아 아버지가 될 때
비로소 자신 속에서 으르렁거리던 짐승과
화해한다
아름다운 어른이 된다

男人们

男人们
生了女儿，成为父亲的时候
终于和身体里咆哮的野兽
诀别
望着女儿的下身
男人知道了神灵之路
醒悟到婴儿出生之地
便是神灵出现的地方
突然因羞愧而脸红
亲吻女儿的时候
他知道自己的胡子有时是毒刺
男人们
生了女儿，成为父亲的时候
终于和身体里咆哮的野兽
和解
成为美丽的大人

For Men

Men,
when they become the father of a new daughter
can finally slip free
of the beasts that growl inside.
Looking at the daughter's vagina,
they realize God's path.
Learning that where the baby comes out
is where God came out
they suddenly blush.
They kiss their daughters,
and know their whiskers can be toxic thorns.
Men
when they become the father of a new daughter
at last make peace
with the beasts that growl inside.
They become lovely adults.

(Translated by Clare You and Richard Silberg)

유방

윗옷 모두 벗기운 채
맨살로 차가운 기계를 끌어안는다
찌그러지는 유두 속으로
공포가 독한 에테르 냄새로 파고든다
패잔병처럼 두 팔 들고
맑은 달 속의 흑점을 찾아
유방암 사진을 찍는다
사춘기 때부터 레이스 헝겊 속에
꼭꼭 싸매 놓은 유방
누구에게나 있지만 항상
여장의 것만 문제가 되어
마치 수치스러운 과일이 달린 듯
깊이 숨겨 왔던 유방
우리의 어머니가 이를 통해
지혜와 사랑을 입에 넣어 주셨듯이
세상의 아이들을 키운 비옥한 대자연의 구릉
다행히 내게도 두 개나 있어 좋았지만
오랫동안 진정 나의 소유가 아니었다
사랑하는 남자의 것이었고
또 아기의 것이었으니까
하지만 나 지금 윗옷 모두 벗기운 채

맨살로 차가운 기계를 안고 서서
이 유방이 나의 것임을 뼈저리게 느낀다
맑은 달 속의 흑점을 찾아
축 늘어진 슬픈 유방을 촬영하며

乳房

上身全部脱光
赤裸裸地抱着冰冷的机器
恐惧散发着强烈的乙醚味
深入干瘪的乳头
像残兵败将高举双手
寻找皎洁月光里的黑点 拍摄乳腺癌照片
从青春期开始就被蕾丝布片
紧紧包裹的乳房
每个人都有
只有女人的乳房存在问题
像结了羞耻的果实
深深隐藏的乳房
我们的母亲通过乳房
把爱和智慧送进我们嘴里
这是大自然哺育世间孩子的肥沃丘陵
幸好我也有两个
很久以来它们并不真正属于我
而属于我爱的男人
和我的孩子
但是此刻，我脱掉上衣
赤裸裸地抱着冰冷的机器

彻骨地感觉到这两个乳房属于我
寻找皎洁月光里的黑点
拍摄低垂的悲伤的乳房

Breasts

Blouse and bra taken off,
I embrace the cold machine.
The strong anxious smell of ethylene
penetrates my crushed breasts.
Both arms raised like a defeated soldier,
I surrender to the mammogram
looking for a moon dark spot.
These breasts wrapped tight in lace
since my teens.
Though everyone has them
only women's are a problem;
like a sheaf of shameful confessions
breasts are kept a deep secret.
Our mothers fed us
wisdom and love though them
fertile hills of mammalian nature.
Fortunately I've owned two but
for a long time they were not mine;
they belonged to my lover
or to my babies.
Stripped now

Naked flesh embracing a machine
I own them to the depth of my bones.
These sad, drooping breasts,
clear moons being probed for dark spots.

(Translated by Clare You and Richard Silberg)

사랑해야 하는 이유

우리가 서로 사랑해야 하는 이유는
세상의 강물을 나눠 마시고
세상의 채소를 나누어 먹고
똑 같은 해와 달 아래
똑 같은 주름을 만들고 산다는 것이라네
우리가 서로 사랑해야 해야 하는
또 하나의 이유는
세상의 강가에서 똑같이
시간의 돌멩이를 던지며 운다는 것이라네
바람에 나뒹굴다가
서로 누군지도 모르는
나뭇잎이나 쇠똥구리 같은 것으로
똑같이 흩어지는 것이라네

爱的理由

我们必须相爱的理由
是共饮人世间的河水
同食人世间的蔬菜
又在相同的太阳和月亮之下
长出同样的皱纹
我们必须相爱的
另一个理由
是我们在人间的河边
抛出岁月的石子，哭泣
我们在风中翻滚
和素不相识的树叶
或屎壳郎一样
飘散

Why We Must Love

We must love each other
because we share the earth's water,
we share the vegetation of the earth.
Under the same sun and moon,
we all wrinkle and grow old.
And we should love each other
because we all cry while throwing time's stones
into the rivers of the earth
We tumble in the wind
without knowing one another.
Like falling leaves or scuttling beetles,
we are all separated and dispersed.

(Translated by Seong Kon Kim and Alec Gordon)

혼자 가질 수 없는 것들

가장 아름다운 것은
손으로 잡을 수 없게 만드셨다
사방에 피어나는
저 나무들과 꽃들 사이
푸르게 솟아나는 웃음 같은 것

가장 소중한 것은
혼자 가질 수 없게 만드셨다
새로 건 달력 속에 숨 쉬는 처녀들
당신의 호명을 기다리는 좋은 언어들

가장 사랑스러운 것은
저절로 솟게 만드셨다
서로를 바라보는 눈 속으로
그윽이 떠오르는 별 같은 것

一个人无法拥有的事物

您让最美丽的事物
无法抓在手里
比如四周
树木和花朵之间
冒出的绿油油的笑

您让最宝贵的事物
无法独自拥有
比如新日历上呼吸的女孩
等待您呼唤的美好的言语

您让最可爱的事物
自动涌现
比如互相对视的眼睛里
悄然升起的星星

What We Cannot Own

The most beautiful thing isn't meant to be touched—
a dazzling smile blooming
among flower and trees.

The most precious thing aren't meant to be owned—
calendar photos of gorgeous girls,
the memory of fine poetic words.

The loveliest thing isn't meant to hidden—
the light that shines in lovers' eyes
as they gaze at one another.

(Translated by Seong Kon Kim and Alec Gordon)

作者简介

文贞姬，韩国诗人，东国大学讲座教授，曾获现代文学奖、素月诗歌奖、郑芝溶文学奖、瑞典“蝉”国际文学奖等。2004年凭诗集《喷泉》获马其顿泰托沃世界文学论坛年度诗人奖。2008年获韩国艺术评论家协会年度最优秀艺术家奖。曾参加美国爱荷华大学国际写作计划。英译诗集有*Windflower*、*Woman on the Terrace*及*I Must Be the Wind*。

Moon Chung-hee (South Korea) is a poet and Endowed Chair Professor at Dongguk University. She has won prestigious awards such as the Sowol Poetry Award, the Chong Chi-Yong Literature Prize, the Mogwol Literature Prize, and Sweden's Cikada Prize. She has participated in the International Writing Program at the University of Iowa. English editions of her books include *Windflower, Woman on the Terrace,* and *I Must Be the Wind.*

图书在版编目（CIP）数据

在机场写信：朝、汉、英 /（韩）文贞姬著；薛舟译. -- 南京：江苏凤凰文艺出版社，2021.1

（红狐丛书. 一衣带水的相望）

ISBN 978-7-5594-1387-1

Ⅰ. ①在… Ⅱ. ①文… ②薛… Ⅲ. ①诗集－韩国－现代－朝鲜语、汉语、英语 Ⅳ. ①I312.625

中国版本图书馆CIP数据核字（2019）第160948号

红狐丛书·一衣带水的相望：在机场写信

北岛 主编

（韩）文贞姬 著

薛舟 译

出 版 人 张在健

责任编辑 王娱瑶 于奎潮

特约编辑 薛 倩 傅春晖

书籍设计 周伟伟

责任印制 刘 巍

出版发行 江苏凤凰文艺出版社

南京市中央路165号，邮编：210009

出版社网址 http://www.jswenyi.com

印 刷 苏州越洋印刷有限公司

开 本 880×1230毫米 1/32

印 张 2.25

字 数 20千字

版 次 2021年1月第1版

印 次 2021年1月第1次印刷

标准书号 ISBN 978-7-5594-1387-1

定 价 128.00元（全七册）